INSPIRE HONOR

INSPIRE HONOR

Inspiring Writings About Honor

Anthology 2023

EDITED BY

DEBRA CELOVSKY

AND

ROBYNNE ELIZABETH MILLER

INSPIRE HONOR

Copyright © 2023 Inspire Christian Writers. Individual pieces within this anthology are copyrights of the authors.

All rights reserved. No part of this publication may be reproduced, distributed, translated, or transmitted in any form or by any means, including photocopying, recording, or other electronic or mechanical methods, without the prior written permission of the author, except in the case of brief quotations embodied in critical reviews and certain other noncommercial uses permitted by copyright law.

ISBN 978-1-938196-22-5

Scripture quotations taken from the Amplified® Bible (AMP), Copyright © 2015 by The Lockman Foundation. Used by permission. lockman.org.

Scripture quotations marked (ESV) are taken from The ESV® Bible (The Holy Bible, English Standard Version®), copyright © 2001 by Crossway, a publishing ministry of Good News Publishers. Used by permission. All rights reserved.

Scripture quotations marked (NASB) are taken from the (NASB®) New American Standard Bible®, Copyright © 1960, 1971, 1977, 1995, 2020 by The Lockman Foundation. Used by permission. All rights reserved. www.lockman.org

Scripture quotations marked (NIV) are taken from the Holy Bible, New International Version®, NIV®. Copyright © 1973, 1978, 1984, 2011 by Biblica, Inc.™ Used by permission of Zondervan. All rights reserved worldwide. www.zondervan.com. The "NIV" and "New International Version" are trademarks registered in the United States Patent and Trademark Office by Biblica, Inc.™

Scripture quotations marked (NKJV) are taken from the New King James Version®. Copyright © 1982 by Thomas Nelson. Used by permission. All rights reserved.

Scripture quotations marked (NLT) are taken from the Holy Bible, New Living Translation, copyright ©1996, 2004, 2015 by Tyndale House Foundation. Used by permission of Tyndale House Publishers, Carol Stream, Illinois 60188. All rights reserved.

Cover designed by Lainey La Shay
Interior design & layout by Author Digital Services
Published by Inspire Christian Writers

Dedication

This anthology is dedicated to those who have
demonstrated honor in all its many forms.
To an ideal, a person, to their own beliefs . . . or to God.

This collection is also dedicated to the amazing
membership of Inspire Christian Writers.
Their dedication to honoring God through the use of gifts
He's equipped them with, and the resulting stories of
honor those gifts produce, encourages and uplifts us.

Be devoted to one another in love.
Honor one another above yourselves
(Romans 12:10, NIV).

Special thanks to:

Debra Celovsky
Robynne E. Miller
Ian Feavearyear
The entire editorial team
(What an honor to work with you all!)
Lainey La Shay, cover artist extraordinaire
And the board of directors of Inspire Christian Writers
Without all of you, this project
would never have happened.

Thank you.

Contents

INSPIRE HONOR

Introduction

The concept of **honor** seems to have slipped from our culture's vocabulary. And behavior. We no longer seem terribly worried about being an honor to our families, friends, or our God. Where once we would have given deference to elders, teachers, parents, bosses, etc., we now think far more about our own needs and wants and glory.

But God has much to say about the importance of honor . . . showing it . . . demonstrating it . . . and walking in it. Scripture talks about honoring leaders, parents, marriage, each other, and Himself. Why? Because a people who *do* demonstrate and walk in honor reflect Him. What's more, a culture who shows respect and honor to each other, and all the institutions and relationships around us, live richer, fuller, more intentional lives.

God wants the concept of honor to seep into our very DNA. In part, to become more like him. In part, so we love each other in the way He intended: full of Christ-like devotion to each other.

This anthology, a collection of stories, poems, and articles on the subject of honor, written by the members of Inspire Christian Writers, demonstrates the myriad ways honor can, and should, be part of our everyday lives.

We hope you enjoy this anthology. And we hope every entry in this collection points you back to the one we most want to honor: Jesus.

– 1 –

Climbing Toward Honor

Lainey La Shay

Dad's old red suburban bounced and jolted over the rocky ravines of Forest Road 189 as we followed a line of cars toward the Grays Peak trailhead. The first rays of sunshine had yet to touch the dense evergreen forest, and we could see only as far as our headlights. Every now and again, a branch scraped against the side of Dad's truck. A spray of stars stretched overhead in a clear velvet sky.

We rolled into the packed parking lot just shy of five o'clock in the morning, scoring the last available parking space. Despite the recent August heat wave, the temperatures here in the Rocky Mountains were crisp and cool. A few gulps of the fresh mountain air washed away the green tint in our cheeks from the bumpy ride and replaced it with the flush of exhilaration.

The five of us crowded around the rear of the suburban as we bundled up in a few extra layers and hoisted our hiking packs. Dad and Mom, my brother Ryan, his beautiful bride, Andi, and I, all converged on Colorado, traveling from all corners of the country to be here today and honor my mom's journey.

Mom fidgeted with her Osprey® backpack, one we'd broken in during a hike in the Cascades a few months before. She fumbled with her hiking poles as if this was the first time she'd ever used them. And while it wasn't her first hike, not by a long stretch, today did mark a first. This was her first attempt at climbing a fourteener.

"You're not nervous, are you?" I teased as I helped her adjust the poles to the correct height. Dad helped her with her backpack, tucking some pads under the shoulder straps to keep them from rubbing.

She laughed and glanced over her shoulder to where the 14,278-foot mountain sat cloaked by the waning night. "I can't believe I'm doing this. What am I thinking?"

"You're thinking you're going to honor all that hard

work you've put into training for this," Ryan said as he held Delia's leash. The dog's long brown fur flopped into her eyes as she woofed her agreement.

"You've worked so hard to get here," Andi agreed. "Besides, you need to honor what God's put on your heart." A smile spread across my lips as I studied my mom, decked out in her hiking gear.

"That I do." Her hand, beginning to show signs of arthritis, patted her zippered pocket where she carried something special. "Can we pray before we start? I think I'm going to need all the help I can get to climb this mountain today."

We joined in a circle and prayed for strength, safety, and joy on the climb, and Mom asked me to anoint her. Tears brimmed in her eyes as she mustered the courage to take the first steps toward the trailhead and honor the journey God had set before her.

"Are we ready?" My father, an avid hiker, surveyed each of us to ensure we weren't missing any necessary gear for the seven-mile climb.

"Ready!"

We squeezed into a group selfie at the trailhead, crossed a wooden bridge that ran over a bubbling creek, and set foot on the rocky trail. Step by step, climbing upward from the forest into alpine terrain, Mom balanced on her hiking poles and pushed forward.

The trail evened out as the sun came over the ridge behind us and flooded the valley with golden light. Fields of columbine and Indian paintbrush burst into color as they turned their petals toward the light. Grays Peak, and its neighbor, Torreys Peak, were bathed in rosy pink sunshine.

As the trail reached the base of Grays Peak, it began to wind upward through scattered talus fields. Mom hesitated as she faced the boulder fields. She swallowed and squared her shoulders, taking one careful step at a time, afraid to fall, but determined not to fail.

"You've got this, Momma," I said from behind her, a hand ready in case she stumbled.

But halfway up the mountain, she froze, staring down at the steep ravine to her right and the vertical mile ahead. She wiped her brow. "I don't think I can do this. This isn't how I thought it would be."

Ryan came bounding back down the trail toward her. "You didn't expect a paved walk in the park, now, did you?"

"Well, no. But I didn't expect all these rocks."

We laughed. "Minor inconveniences." My brother waved his hand. "You're almost there."

I sneaked Mom some jellybeans from the stash I always kept in my pocket when hiking. The sweet treat lifted her mood and gave her energy between snack breaks.

"One rock at a time, Momma."

The higher we climbed up the peak, the more the view expanded. Rolling ridges and alpine hills carpeted in flowers stretched in all directions. Clouds raced through the endless blue sky on invisible air currents, swirling around the other peaks. The temperature began to drop, and so did the amount of oxygen.

Each step became more difficult, and we took two breaths for every one we had taken at the trailhead. Ryan, Andi, and Delia scouted the trail ahead, showing Mom the best path to take through the summit boulder field. Delia raced back and forth, making sure Mom was still climbing. Dad and I brought up the rear.

"Push me up the hill," Mom teased. I reached out one finger, pressing it to her back and "pushing." She laughed, momentarily forgetting the struggle. "You know, I've always wanted to do this. All those times you and your dad were out hiking and climbing mountains, I wanted to be there so much I'd sit at home and cry. But my knees and balance were so bad, and my weight was out of control. I knew I couldn't do it."

"But look at you now. You have lost all that weight—over a hundred and fifty pounds!—you've gotten your knees replaced, and you've been working so hard with your coach for over a year. You always said you'd never run a half marathon, but you did it. And now look at you. You never thought you'd climb a fourteener, but you're going to conquer it. See? The summit is just right there."

Her face lit up with determination, and she dug her hiking poles into the ground. She put one foot in front of the other, summiting the mountain and thrusting her hiking poles into the air with a cheer.

Clouds rolled over the summit and the wind gusted. Our group pulled on every layer of clothing we had packed and hunkered down behind a low makeshift wall to eat some lunch—tuna on crackers, apples, and rice—while discussing the climb. We were on the tenth highest peak in the Rockies, but Mom was on top of the world.

As our group picked our way over the summit boulders toward the trail, ready to return to lower altitudes, Mom pulled a small turquoise container from her pocket. It was round and transparent, holding a tri-toned cross necklace she had purchased at the store.

I stepped up beside her as she studied the glimmering cross. "God has given me so much, and has blessed me with my family, restored health, and a great life. It hasn't been easy. In fact, sometimes I wondered if I'd ever make it through. So, I'm going to leave this here. I feel like God wants me to leave it for someone I may never meet, but who needs to know Him, or that He will help them conquer the mountains in their life, too."

Mom kneeled down and tucked the container between the rocks where we had eaten lunch, leaving just enough turquoise peeking out for it to be visible.

As she did, the clouds that had been swirling around the summit parted, and a band of sunlight broke through, illuminating the ground where she had placed the cross. The turquoise gleamed. Mom laughed, and tears sprang to her eyes. "It's like God is honoring my journey and what I've just done."

"I think He is." I wrapped my arm around her shoulders. "I'm proud of you."

We began the descent through the boulder field and down winding switchbacks. Ryan and Dad debated hiking the ridge and summiting Torreys Peak, but changed plans as a summer squall rolled through the pass, dropping rain and pea-sized hail. The storm passed as quickly as it had begun, and the air warmed.

We reached the trailhead, and exhausted tears streamed down Mom's face.

"You did it, Momma!" The five of us huddled into a group hug, Delia barking in celebration. What a joy to witness Mom honoring herself and her Lord on the mountain.

"Which fourteener are you going to climb next?" Ryan asked.

Mom laughed. "Oh, heck no. I'm one and done."

"Well, never say never."

– 2 –

Honor to His Name

Robyn Mulder

"You'll bring honor to us all!"

That's the catchy line from the first song in the movie *Mulan*.

From the very beginning of this story, we realize that honor is of utmost importance in Chinese society. Poor Mulan is forced to dress up and try to act a certain way before she meets with the matchmaker. The song explains that girls are expected to become tiny-waisted, calm, and obedient wives if they want to bring honor to their families.

Her mother waits impatiently for Mulan to show up, and then Grandma gives her a lucky cricket so she doesn't blow it.

But the meeting with the matchmaker doesn't go well at all. Mulan can't remember her lines, she spills the tea, and she has trouble keeping her unruly cricket under control. Chaos ensues, and the scene ends with the matchmaker screaming, "You may *look* like a bride, but you will never bring your family honor!"

Most people know the rest of the story: Mulan decides to disguise herself as a man so she can take her father's place in the war against the Huns. She fights valiantly, but when her ruse is discovered, she is sent home in disgrace. Later, she returns to the fight—fully herself—and helps to save the emperor. She does bring honor to her family, just not in the traditional way. She brings them honor when she lives authentically and doesn't try to hide who she is.

I can't help thinking of my own life as a Christian when I think of Mulan's story. I want my family to be proud of me, of course, but I don't feel the pressure to bring honor to them. Instead, my focus is centered on God.

I used to think honoring God looked a certain way. I thought I had to be perfect and never make mistakes if I wanted to bring Him honor. Like poor Mulan, I could never be good enough and I wallowed in regret and shame every time I failed.

Even worse, I listened as Satan screamed accusations at me: "You may *look* like a Christian on the outside but look at how messed up you are on the inside. You'll never honor God that way!"

Believing Satan's condemnation and the lies in my own head kept me fearful and worried for many years. How could I honor God if I kept messing up? Why even try if I couldn't be perfect?

In recent years I've finally been able to recognize the thoughts in my head as terrible lies that stop me from accepting myself and prevent me from honoring the God I love with all my heart.

The Holy Spirit has been showing me that God has a way of using people's messes to bring glory and honor to Himself.

Just think of everyone in the Bible who failed and still brought God glory.

Adam and Eve sinned in Eden, but God still loved them after they were exiled from the garden.

Jonah disobeyed God and tried to go in the opposite direction of Nineveh, but God sent a fish to save him. The city of Nineveh repented after Jonah's preaching.

David committed adultery with Bathsheba and had her husband killed, but God called him a man after His own heart.

Peter denied Jesus three times, but Jesus restored

their relationship and built His church on Peter.

Saul, later named Paul, persecuted Christians, but Jesus met him on the road to Damascus and called him to preach the good news to both Jews and Gentiles.

Reading the Bible and looking around at the Christians I know have taught me that I can honor God by being myself—mistakes and all. I don't have to change my personality and try to fit in and be like everyone around me.

He loves the way I look. He loves the way I talk. He loves my quirky sense of humor. And He loves it when I point others to Him. He can be honored when I turn to Him during hard times and give Him the glory for any successes I have.

Peter even tells us about the honor that can be the result of suffering through trials of all kinds:

> In all this you greatly rejoice, though now for a little while you may have had to suffer grief in all kinds of trials. These have come so that the proven genuineness of your faith—of greater worth than gold, which perishes even though refined by fire—may result in praise, glory and honor when Jesus Christ is revealed (1 Peter 1:6–7 NIV).

We may feel grief when we go through trials. We may feel shame when we sin. We may feel regret when we make a mistake and hurt someone we love.

But we can also feel joy when we persevere through hard times. We can feel healthy pride when we repent and turn from our sins. We can feel happiness when we make amends and restore a relationship.

We honor God when we do all those things. His name is glorified when people see us living an authentic, honest life. Even when we make a mess of things.

We don't need a lucky cricket. We just need the Holy Spirit's guidance and a commitment to love the Lord with all our heart, soul, mind, and strength. Imperfectly, but sincerely.

So, let's live like that. "We'll bring honor to His name!"

– 3 –

Honoring the Dishonorable

Christine Hagion

On a busy day at work, with hundreds of details about the event I was planning for the following week swirling in my mind, I was completely unprepared for the news.

The phone rang, and I answered absentmindedly while typing on my keyboard. A familiar voice greeted me.

"Hello, Christy." I recognized the deep voice belonging to Larry, my eldest brother, whom I'd not seen for two decades. His calling me out of the blue was unusual. Our family members, scattered all over the country, did not keep in touch.

"What a surprise!" I smiled. "What's the occasion that you're calling me at the office?" *And how did he find out where I worked?* I wondered.

"I have some bad news," he began.

Well, whatever it is, I don't have time for it right now, with this event at work coming up.

"Okay. So, what's this earth-shattering news that's so important you'd call in the middle of a workday?"

"Maters died." Maters, Larry's nickname for my mother.

"Jeepers! We were going to visit her again in two months. I already made the lodging reservations." It'd become our annual family "vacation," to take a week off and make the eleven-hour trek to Oregon to visit Maters in her assisted living facility.

I recalled our first visit after the incident that could've taken my daughter's life. My husband had driven myself, my two daughters, and his mother in our comfortable minivan. Maters had never met my spouse or children. I'd been shocked but not surprised at her appearance: because of her half-century habit of smoking, she was more wrinkled than her years alone would've produced. Creases were chiseled into her face, and she was thinner than I'd ever seen her. She walked into the patio, aided by the nursing staff, and the nurse pulled a wheeled tank of oxygen behind

Maters. After settling her into a lawn chair and securing the canister, the nurse cautioned Maters not to light her cigarette until the oxygen was turned off so she wouldn't blow us all up.

Not the greatest impression on my mother-in-law. But she was cordial and kind as she spoke to Maters, making polite conversation to a woman her junior by over a decade, but whom by all appearances could've been twenty years her senior. I'd been embarrassed by Maters, as usual. Just as I had since grade school.

We'd parted ways years before, when I was a single mother and my eldest child, Karis, was a preschooler. Maters had blown into town, a decade after I'd seen her last, showing up unexpectedly at my job. I'd allowed her to stay in my apartment, provided she remained sober. She lived with us for a few months, and she'd loved reading children's books aloud with Karis on her lap. We'd joined Maters, at her request, at a Thanksgiving dinner hosted by her AA group. Later, we enjoyed a modest Christmas celebration together.

However, one night I came home to my unlit apartment and deposited my keys, calling her name into the darkness. I finally found Maters upstairs, passed out on Karis's bed. Beside Maters on the nightstand was the remnant of a cigarette she'd laid down on the bare wood, its long ash evidence that it'd been placed there while still lit. Thankfully it had burned itself out and hadn't taken Karis's bedroom furniture up with it. *I could've come home to a raging fire engulfing my home because of her carelessness,* I thought.

I brewed a fresh pot of coffee, although it was nearly midnight. I tried waking Maters, but she was out cold. Again. *How many times has this happened over the years?* I'd found her unconscious from drinking countless times in my youth.

Our discussion of her actions would have to wait until the morning.

I put Karis to sleep in my bed and maintained my guard. I would not give in to exhaustion or allow myself much-needed rest. I watched through the night so that if Maters awoke from her stupor, she would not repeat her stupid mistake while we slept and have us roasting in flames.

When her eyes opened lazily, I said, "Pack your things. You're leaving today."

"Wait. I gotta wake up."

"I'll get you a cup of coffee and a bus ticket out of town. You are no longer welcome in this house."

"Why?"

"Do you even have to ask? I warned you when you first came that you could only stay if you weren't drinking again. Your alcoholism destroyed my life. I won't let you destroy my daughter's, too."

The pain on her face told me that my words had struck their target.

"Look at the nightstand. You could've burned my place down last night. It's not like I don't have ashtrays, but you were too drunk to care. I don't want to hurt you, but I must protect my daughter."

I'd not seen Maters again until our visit at the assisted living facility, when she'd sat in the patio with an oxygen cannula under her nose, breathing out obscenities and cigarette smoke. I'd struggled for years with balancing the scriptural mandate to honor a mother who was anything but honorable. I'd reasoned that, in this controlled environment, she couldn't do harm to my family, so visiting her was my way of trying to do so. The only way I knew how.

"Since you're the closest of us all, I think you should go and attend to her remains." My brother's voice on the phone jolted me out of the unpleasant memories.

"Yes, yes, of course I should." I, the youngest of the five children, had always been the one who'd taken responsibility for cleaning up my mother's messes. I didn't blame the others for fleeing the madness as soon as they could. *But wait. I have this big event at work next week. How can I do that?*

My thoughts pivoted. I had a million details to attend to, tasks to delegate to the team, and a trip to plan. I made lists, phone calls, and spoke to Janet, my boss, announcing my imminent departure due to my mother's unexpected death.

"Wow. Your mother dying. You must be so torn up about it," Janet said while grabbing my hand, trying to be supportive.

Nope. I resigned myself to this a long time ago. "I have a lot of details to hammer out before I can go, and I'll have to manage it quickly and return in time for next week's event." I replied without volunteering details.

"You should be crying and mourning her loss," Janet said. *I've been mourning her for years. I'm all cried out. And who are you to tell me how I should grieve for someone who's caused me nothing but grief my whole life?*

"Now's not the time to blub about it. I'm endeavoring to be professional and diligent, ensuring that the event will still take place. Sentimentality will have to wait."

The next day a co-worker came by my desk, tears in her eyes.

"I'm so sorry about your mother," she said, handing me a sympathy card.

Really? I'm not. "Thank you. That is so kind," I'd muttered. *Why are you crying about my mother? If you'd known the devastation and destruction she left in her wake, you'd know she wasn't worth your tears*. As a preteen, I'd told Maters that she loved her booze more than her own children. She'd slapped my face.

Another co-worker brought me a vase of flowers. "To help you with your grief," she said. *Grief is what I lived and breathed for decades because of her misdeeds, which were too numerous to count*. Though I'd forgiven her, the pain of a lost childhood lingered.

On our most recent visit, the previous year, Maters had obviously been declining. She'd been bedridden in a nursing home, and both Karis and I had known that this was probably the last time we'd see her alive. That must've been the Holy Spirit informing me of what was to come.

On the phone, I conversed with the doctor who'd pronounced Maters dead. He reported she had ten different diagnoses, most of which contributed to her demise. We made plans for me to obtain the death certificate once I arrived up north. I e-mailed everyone on my team, leaving specific instructions on tasks to follow up on, and my cell phone number for a conference call in two days' time to ensure that the event would go smoothly once I returned.

In Oregon, after arranging her cremation, I sorted through her belongings. Among them was an audiotape

I'd sent recording all of us singing Christmas carols and sending well wishes to Maters for the holidays. Also, a scrapbook I'd made for her with pictures of her adult children and grandchildren, most of whom she'd never met.

Honor your father and your mother, the commandment declares (Deut. 5:16 NKJV). Given the circumstances, I honored Maters the best I could.

– 4 –

The Big Picture

Adrienne N. Wartts

During our free day while attending a writers' retreat on Martha's Vineyard, Brenda, one of the writers, called to ask if I wanted to go to the thrift shop in Vineyard Haven. "Sure, I can meet you after I take pictures of the gingerbread cottages," I said. "It's early, so this is a good time to get photos without people in them."

Brenda laughed. "What's wrong with taking pictures with people in them?"

"Well, nothing is wrong with it, but who needs a photographer in today's world where people are obsessed with taking selfies," I said. "I can look at people anytime, but the only time I can see the beauty of the island is when I'm here."

She laughed again. "All right. We've got to get you to like people. What's a good time to meet up to go to the thrift shop?"

After we agreed on a time, I draped my camera around my neck and strapped my black Nautica® purse full of lenses across my chest. I then walked along the pier. As I was heading toward Circuit Avenue, there were about twenty-five people standing on the ramp of a restaurant called Biscuits. Everyone looked happy. They were chatting, laughing, and embracing each other. One man was trying to organize everyone.

Each person was dressed in white attire except for one young woman who wore a red plaid shirt and jeans. The men sported white suits, the women wore white dresses or ivory slacks and blouses, and all the children had on white ensembles. The family prepared for the pose and one of the restaurant employees took a photo with a mobile device.

As I was passing by, one of the young women smiled. "Oh, a professional photographer! I wish you could take a picture of us," she said. "We are celebrating my aunt's sixtieth birthday, and I would love to have a professional photo. I'll pay for it."

Even though I did not feel confident in my ability to take a high-quality photo, I agreed to do it. "You don't have to pay me. I'll be glad to take a photo." I then immediately thought to myself, *Oh, geez ... what did I just say and what have I just gotten myself into?*

Just then, a more senior woman from the group joined our interaction. "Yeah, she's a professional photographer. Look at her. She's got the Nikon®, a camera bag, and everything."

As the group assembled for another picture, I turned toward the pier and sighed as I laughed about God's three messengers and His sense of humor. Then I took a few photos.

The Bible says, *Each of you should use whatever gift you have received to serve others, as faithful stewards of God's grace in its various forms* (1 Peter 4:10 NIV). While I planned to bask in the beauty of colorful homes, I was prompted to look at the big picture.

The big picture required me to listen to the Holy Spirit and honor God's plans as to how He desired me to use my gift of photography in that present moment. While I had planned to take photos of inanimate objects, God prompted me to honor a family by using my camera to help them capture and preserve a special occasion. He orchestrated the opportunity by having me pass by the family gathering with my camera on display at a precise moment. And even though I was not comfortable with the task when I spontaneously agreed to take the photo, God gave me grace.

– 5 –

Clothed in Honor

Anita Peluso

Anya attempted to counter her opponent's strike, but her arm grew tired, causing her sword to narrowly miss its mark. "*Aaahhh!*" she screamed into the wind. "Why must my aim always fail?"

Her adversary, Sigrid, stepped back, her own weapon at her side, and laughed at Anya. "The answer is simple. I am better at the sword," she boasted. "You have not logged as many hours in battle, nor do you fight without a care. If you want to slay your enemy, you must not care about the outcome—theirs or yours."

Anya crossed her arms and paced in front of the

Meister overseeing their training. It was true—she did care about the outcome. She could not slay a foe simply because they were her enemy. *Was life not more than winning or losing a battle? Did not the God of the Holy Scriptures say that He took no pleasure in the death of the wicked?*

"You fight like a child who does not trust her sword," taunted Sigrid.

How can I trust in my sword when it so often misses its mark? Try as she might, she could not get the sword and her body to work as one.

"Again," commanded the Meister.

Anya raised her weapon, drew the sign of a cross in the air, and took a fighting stance. Sigrid quickly sliced through the air once with her sword, raised it to shoulder height, and stood with her feet apart.

"You cannot defeat me, Anya," Sigrid smirked.

Anya searched Sigrid's eyes for that flickering squint or faint tightening of muscles that would indicate the intent of her opponent's next move. *You may be right, but winning is not my goal.*

Sigrid lunged forward, swinging her sword toward Anya.

Anya side-stepped to the left as Sigrid's blade slashed the air, missing its mark. Sigrid spun around to face Anya again, looking for an opening to advance.

Intent on the match at hand, neither woman heard the soft hiss of an arrow soaring toward their Meister. The sound of a muffled cry followed by gurgling escaped his lips as his body fell to the ground, bringing first Anya, then Sigrid, to a halt.

Anya ran to his side as Sigrid surveyed the edge of the meadow where they practiced. The sunlight filtering through the leaves made the shadows dance. Several seconds passed before Sigrid cried out, "Anya, look!"

Twelve strides away among the trees, a half-dozen warriors stood dressed for battle, weapons raised. Four men and two women from a neighboring tribe, who mourned the loss of their brother in a previous battle, now sneered at Sigrid and Anya.

"Toke!" raged Sigrid. "You show yourself to be no son of the Most High by sending an arrow through a man's back."

"My brother's blood cries out for vengeance," shouted the tall, grizzly-faced man in the middle. "The Holy Scriptures demand an eye for an eye, a life for a life!"

"Then the price has been paid by the death of our Meister," Sigrid shouted with anger in her voice.

"The arrow spent on your Meister is but a warning. Face me as the warrior you boast, and then we will see if your debt can be paid."

Toke spoke with a calm confidence that ran shivers down Anya's spine. The air, filled with tension, hung silent as the two parties assessed one another. Which would prevail—the pride and expertise of a well-trained shield maiden, or the confidence fueled by revenge and anger?

"Fine. Then let us settle the debt." The muscles in Sigrid's arms and neck stiffened as she picked up her double-edged sword and faced her opponent. "This match is between you and me. Instruct your soldiers to stand aside."

"I will accede to your terms." Toke expanded his arms outward, signaling his companions to yield.

"Your people will accept the outcome?" Sigrid asked, wondering at Toke's quick agreement.

Toke glowered at Sigrid with a barely perceptible nod of his head.

"You must know your brother lost no honor in his death. Though it was my blade that ended his breath, it was meant for another. Your brother fought valiantly to defend our people against the raiders who ravage our land."

Anya knew that the Holy Scriptures made provision for accidental deaths if it could be proven the strike was unintentional. Sigrid had been found innocent of the death of Toke's brother, but Toke and his band disagreed with the council's ruling. Anya was shocked that Toke would seek revenge against the instructions of the council and the Holy Scriptures.

Toke carried his *ulfberht* low by his side as he paced around the perimeter of the meadow and studied Sigrid's every move. Sigrid held his gaze while gripping the hilt of her blade, pairing her steps to his in readiness.

Moments passed like an eternity as Anya stood rooted near the now-dead Meister. She watched Sigrid and Toke assess each other's strengths and weaknesses, searching for an opportunity to make the first strike.

"Take her," shouted Toke's soldiers. "You can easily finish her!"

With both hands on his sword, Toke suddenly swung at Sigrid, cutting upward across his body, aiming for her face.

Sigrid lurched backward while lifting her sword to meet Toke's blade in mid-air. The tip of his weapon came short of her face by a hand's width as the clash of metal against metal rang out in the silence of the meadow.

Toke recovered quickly and swung his sword downward toward Sigrid's midsection.

Anya gasped at Toke's swift parry.

Sigrid swung with all her might, blocking Toke's blow. The tip of his blade made its connection, grazing her tunic and leaving a trail of red.

Sigrid briefly registered the strike, but her hands remained firm on her weapon as she studied Toke's movements. She swung her sword downward toward Toke's shoulder, cutting a deep gash across his bicep.

Toke raged at the sting of Sigrid's blade and let out a growl. He swung wildly at Sigrid in retaliation.

Sigrid's face turned hard and calculated. Intent on the duel, she blocked each of Toke's blows with swift precision.

As Toke pushed Sigrid backward with his wild swinging, the space between them and Anya—standing frozen in the grass—grew smaller and smaller until they were dangerously close to one another.

Sigrid raised her blade, then brought it down across her body to disarm Toke. He dodged to the side, and her blade slashed across Anya's chest instead. Anya fell to the ground, eyes wide in bewilderment.

Toke's soldiers gasped. The audible sound brought Sigrid and Toke to a standstill.

Sigrid turned to make sense of the situation and saw Anya lying in the middle of a growing pool of red. She rushed to Anya's side with a look of horror on her face.

"Who did this?" Sigrid raged.

"It was your blade," one of the soldiers cried out.

"Nooooo!" Sigrid wailed. She began to weep at the sight of her sparring partner lying on the ground. "Anya! What have I done?"

"You are not responsible," whispered Anya.

"It should be me wounded at the hand of the sword, not you! How am I to live when it is you that I have struck?"

"I forgive you."

Sigrid's tears ran down her face, dropping onto Anya's tunic as she leaned closer to hear Anya's voice.

Toke stood silent behind Sigrid.

Anya saw the anger seep out of Toke's face as her own life seeped out of her body. She listened to Sigrid sob as she began to close her eyes.

Anya choked out her final words, "Honor … the Most … High. Remember … His … holy … Word. Forgive …" before releasing her last breath.

– 6 –

The Guest of Honor

Joyce D. Hightower

Melvin and Alice held the going-away party for Jonny, their son, with me as the guest of honor. After briefly introducing people gathered in the house courtyard from all over Kenya, Melvin invited me to stand beside him amid the applause and cheers from friends and family. Getting visas and school placements did require persistence, but success came at last. Hosted by my mother in the United States, Jonny would soon leave for further studies.

Dorcas, the eldest daughter, rushed in with a flourish and stopped in front of us. She carried an ornate tray with something wrapped in foil, still steaming. Since arriving in Kenya, this was my first such celebration, and I was unsure about what was happening. Melvin, recognizing my confusion, explained that their Kenyan custom was to honor the highest-ranking guest with a rare delight, a delicacy. The word delicacy made my nerves begin to tingle. In other countries, I had never found this to be something I considered good. Fortunately, whatever this "rare delight" was, I felt safe for the moment. He gave instructions for the tray to be placed at my table seat.

The aroma of a roasted goat gave hope. But this was short-lived as his explanation continued: "The goat, slaughtered and roasted for the occasion, is prepared for all the guests to eat to their satisfaction. The head presented on the tray is to be solely enjoyed by you." This brought applause and calls of joy from the crowd.

I closed my eyes and tried to smile, fighting almost overwhelming nausea. They were unaware I had found it impossible to eat a fish with the head intact because of the eyes staring at me. An attempt at a goat head would not end well. To refuse, with a truthful excuse that I did not eat goat heads and would gladly settle for a piece of shoulder or leg, would be a great insult to one of the most powerful men in the area. Opening my eyes, I found everyone looking at me and the air heavy with expectation. I would have to acknowledge the honor with gratitude. I cringed at the thought of people watching me with envy as I ate something I was sure to gag on—or worse—in the process.

Nausea swept over me again. I turned to the side to hide a disgusted look on my face and clear my throat. Was there no way I could get out of this socially alive? How do you say that you don't want an honor? You could say it without words but offer to share it with everyone else until none was left. That would be too obvious. I was backed into a corner with no apparent escape.

I scanned the crowd, searching for an overlooked option. Jonny was leaning against the opposite wall with a group of his friends. His grandma sat in a nearby corner, cupping her hand behind her ear to hear better. There was no more time. The guests were quietly waiting for me to speak.

Thank God words came to me as I spoke: "At times like this, I am reminded that I would not be here if it had not been for my parents. That is not only in the physical sense but also in their love and care for me. They encouraged and guided me. Even though my father is dead, my mother has continued to be a source of inspiration to me. As Jonny is under her wing in the U.S., she will do the same for him. Jonny, you are embarking on a journey that your parents prepared. You are the first of your family to go to the U.S. for school. Your mom and dad deserve greater honor than I do. Let us all honor them."

I gestured for Alice to come and stand beside Melvin and encouraged the guests to stand and applaud. Everyone joyfully did so as the couple beamed with pride.

When the crowd sat again quietly, Melvin reached to shake my hand. I knew he was about to take charge of the occasion again. However, the frantic issue of the goat head was not settled. While shaking his hand, I cleared my throat to continue speaking before he could say anything. He raised his hand to have me pause, but I was determined not to be stuck with the goat head.

"There is another person who deserves even more honor than they do." The room went deadly silent. I knew the fear in everyone's mind was that I was about to insult the host. The rank in order of respect at the few public events I had attended was first the honored guest, then the host, the dignitaries, followed by the other guests. My plan was risky, but I had no other choice.

"Jonny, can I have you escort your grandmother to

the front here? His jaw dropped, and his friends frowned. He hesitated until Melvin nodded his head in consent. He hurried to his grandma and told her she was being called to the front. She waved her hand to be left alone. Melvin whispered to me, "She does not hear or see well. Let me try to convince her."

He walked over to her corner and said something that changed her mind. Steadied by her son and grandson at her sides, she stood and began walking. She arrived in front of the crowd amid applause and cheers in her native tongue. She smiled, surprised but pleased.

As I addressed her, I asked the crowd for silence, speaking slowly to allow Melvin to translate for her. "Grandmother, I was introduced to you earlier as Melvin's mother. I was also told that you raised your son to become a successful businessman after his father died. His vision is to see his son go even further. It's because of *you*, and not me, that Jonny is going to America. So, with great pride, I request that you be the one to enjoy the goat head. You are the one who started the process and faithfully supported it for many years. You are the true guest of honor."

I gestured for everyone to stand again. She did a little hop from sheer joy, and the crowd roared with delight. They cheered and applauded until she held her wrinkled, shaking hand up for quiet. She told Melvin, "Please tell this teacher from America that I have never been the guest of honor in my entire life. I have never met a woman from America."

She chuckled, and others laughed with her.

Addressing the crowd, she said, "As a child, I had few chances to taste what was left of the goat head. I never dreamed that the opportunity to be the one to unwrap and take the first bite would be my pleasure. My eyes no longer see clearly, and my ears miss many things. I have never seen love so clearly or heard wisdom so well as I feel with my heart today." Tears were running down her face as her voice cracked. "I thank her and pray God's blessing on her. Now, I need to sit and enjoy my meal." A roar of laughter spread over the courtyard.

As Jonny and Alice escorted Grandma back to her corner, I signaled Dorcas to put the tray with the goat head on the table before her grandmother.

"Teacher, you have taught us a great lesson today," Melvin said, wiping his tears away. "We assure honor for ourselves when we honor the sacrifices of our elders. Thank you. We will find the tastiest part of the roasted leg meat to serve you in replacement."

Sighing with relief, I sat and enjoyed the rest of the party. I watched from a distance as Grandmother happily ate the goat head, grinned, and frequently raised her hands to thank me.

Several months later, Jonny's grandmother died. Melvin told me she had mentioned with great pride and joy to every visitor we received that she had been presented with the goat head. "It was a life highlight for her. I never saw her as happy or proud as she was that day. We will not have the chance to honor my mother so again. Thank God that you allowed us to do it then."

I am grateful for not having to eat or see the goat head. However, more than that, I am thankful for the lesson that difficult situations often allow us to look for ways to honor others. We may find a chance to give someone honor that not only gets us out of a sticky spot, but also serves to enrich the lives around us. The minimal cost of speaking words of honor to those who have sacrificed for others makes us all richer by far.

– 7 –

A Prayer for Honoring God

Terrie Hellard-Brown

Lord, I honor You with my thoughts.
I ask You to renew my mind.
Help me guard my thoughts, taking them captive,
So they may obey You.
May the meditations of my heart honor You.

Lord, I honor You with my words.
You are the Most High God,
All-powerful, all-knowing, forever faithful, and loving.
You are my God, my Lord, my Savior, and I love You.
May the words from my lips honor You.

Lord, I honor You with my actions.
You are my strength Who guides my steps.
May I be Your hands and feet to those around me.
Help me minister in Your power and bear fruit in
  Your Name.
May the works of my hands honor You.

Lord, I honor You with my life.
I count all as lost.
To live is Christ; to die is gain.
Every choice I make, every breath I take,
May my life bring honor to Your name.
Amen.

out for her."

The experienced missionary lifted his head from under the hood of the engine. "Yes, she can come, if you will look after her, Larry." He replaced the dip-stick with a satisfied grunt. "The lorry is all ready to go."

"Yippee!" I wrinkled my nose. "I get to go with Daddy in the *lorry*." Dad leaned in my window and winked, knowing I liked the local British term for truck.

Once again, I settled into the driver's seat and returned to our imaginary jungle journey. Biting my lip, I concentrated on steering the jerking giant over the rough West African terrain. Larry patiently waited his turn to take over the steering wheel.

Early the next morning, Dad, Larry, and I let out on the once-a-month preaching circuit.

First, we drove to a chapel where two dozen students from the high school jumped in the back of the lorry and sat on planks that stretched across as benches. Mr. Adeyemi, one of the teachers and a good friend of my dad, called out a cheerful greeting "*E karo.* Mr. Jones. Good morning, sir. Thank you for driving us." And he hopped on, too.

Dad steered carefully over washed-out roads through tall savanna grass and on into the jungle. Mile after mile the tires sprayed so much dirt on the outside of the lorry that soon the white paint turned reddish-brown.

Along the way, at a dozen stops, smiling villagers gathered, and two or three of the young men hopped off to lead a Sunday School class and preach in the church. We continued to Omi, the last village on the rutted route.

There we were greeted by a large group of church-goers in front of a white-washed cement building with its metal pan roof. We took our seats on wooden, backless benches. The singing started and everyone joined in. Then my dad stood up and began preaching in English while his good friend, Mr. Adeyemi, translated into Yoruba.

Though the window shutters stood wide open, not even a tiny breeze blew in. Sweat drops tickled my forehead and underarms.

Six or seven village children sat on the floor around me. Giggling and patting my arms, they chanted, "*Oyinbo*! *Oyinbo*!"

I shifted closer to Larry and sat as stiff as a palm tree.

He hugged my waist and whispered in my ear. "*Oyinbo* means 'white man' or 'peeled man.' Now they know girls can have white skin, too."

He waved at the kids to stop touching me. Then, he took a piece of notepaper out of his Bible, folded it in half, and fanned my sweaty face.

Soon all the children moved to sit with their parents. My kind brother sketched an airplane on paper for me. He handed me the pencil and said, "Here, you try it." Larry was good at drawing, but my scribbles looked more like a half-peeled banana than a plane.

For two hours we sat on the hard bench. I got fidgety.

At last, Dad said, "Now, I'll close in prayer."

The villagers filed out the door with smiles, hugs, and happy greetings for Dad. "*A dupe*, thank you, Mr. Jones. Thank you for bringing God's words to us." Then they followed the winding path through the trees to their homes.

Dad unpacked our lunch under the cool, leafy shade of a mango tree next to the church. We had a fun picnic while sitting on the blanket eating SPAM® sandwiches and carrot sticks. My brother dug around in the dirt, hunting for beetles.

After my dad talked with a few more villagers for a while, we began the return drive home. At each small town, we stopped, and the students climbed over the tailgate, telling their stories about preaching the gospel and leading the activities in each community. When we arrived back at the church, each student shook Dad's hand and hugged him the way Nigerian men show friendship.

That evening Mom served us chicken soup and we excitedly told her, little Mark, and baby Grant about the drive, church service, and picnic. I quickly slurped a bowl of our tasty meal.

After supper, I shuffled to my bath and then to my bedroom, tired but happy. By the dim light of our kerosene lamp, I pulled on my short-sleeved pajama top and shorts. I smiled. *At last, I got to go on the Sunday trek with Daddy through the jungle.*

When my dad came in and sat on the edge of my bed, I wrapped my arms around his neck and breathed deeply. I loved the smell of spice he wore after his shower. "I'm so glad I got to go with you today," I said.

Dad kissed my forehead. "It was a long, hot, dusty journey. Are you sure it didn't wear you out?"

I snuggled into my pillow. "Well, I guess I'm tired. But I get lonely when you go without me!"

As I drifted off to sleep, I dreamed of my next adventure in Yorubaland with Dad. My imagination careened down a rocky road while I madly steered the large, white lorry through the Nigerian jungle.

* * *

During the sixteen years I lived in Nigeria, time with my dad was rare because demands of the ministry often took him away from home. In the faraway country that became our homeland, my hard-working father sacrificed much for his family and the Nigerian people. Today, I honor him with gratitude for his steadfast dedication to both.

– 9 –

Again

Janelle Roselli

The sun has yet to rise,
Yet she hears the pattering of feet.
Another sleepless night,
But still, there are mouths to feed.
Laundry to be done,
Dishes to be cleaned,
Another thankless day,
Yet countless are their needs.
She knows it's God's strength that upholds her,
So, while the baby sleeps, she opens up her Bible and begins to read.
Again.

Another wracking spasm,
He holds her through the pain.
Another doctor's visit,
Another plea for change.
Another day of serving,
Another diagnosis unnerving.
His heart is breaking,
His hands are shaking,
But his faith is unwavering.
He knows that God is good,
So, he lifts his voice in praise and begins to give thanks.
Again.

God's called her to the life of writing,
She heard it loud and clear.
Yet another query returns rejected,
Another unpublished year.
Another "This is good, but not for me,"
Another "You need a greater following."
But she knows this is what she was created to be,
So, she pours herself a cup of coffee and begins typing.
Again.

Honor can be earned by doing lofty deeds,
But let us not overlook the daily opportunities
To sacrifice oneself,
To stand by those in need,
To step into our calling,
Daily, in the hidden things,
In the secret caverns of our souls,
The spaces the world does not see.
So, let us honor God, who deserves the glory,
And trust Him with our story.
Again and again and again.

– 10 –

Broken Crayons

Maureen Miller

My sacrifice, O God, is a broken spirit; a broken and contrite heart you, God, will not despise (Psalm 51:17 NIV).

My little friend sat at the dining table flipping through a coloring book, determining which picture to color.

After several moments, he pointed to a page. "This one," he exclaimed, grinning from ear to ear.

I carefully tore the page from the book, then laid it flat on the wooden surface. "There you go, Buddy! Now, let me get the crayons."

I returned with a colorful tin—the same crayon container I used as a girl. The faces of cartoon-style jungle creatures brought a smile as I placed the tin on the table. "Okay, get busy!"

The little boy reached his hand in and pulled out a

fistful of crayons in a variety of colors. Spreading them out, he considered which one to choose first, but I noticed his hesitation. What he said next confirmed his concern.

"Lots of these are broken," he complained, shoving several colorful nubs aside.

Tousling the top of his head, I chuckled. "It's okay, Buddy. Broken crayons still color."

He looked up at me, uncertainty etched in the lines of his forehead. "Really?"

"Sure thing. Why don't you give it a try?"

And true to my word, a bright blue streak appeared on the page, and, once more, my young friend smiled.

***

Broken crayons still color.

I have a mug that reminds me of this truth—reminding me, too, of all the examples of broken men and women, both in the Bible as well as throughout history, whom God used to color the world.

Think about it. Heroes of the faith, living and long gone—imperfect vessels who served and sacrificed. Fought and failed. Fought and succeeded. Fought for their freedom. For others' freedom. Fought for their faith. Fought despite fear.

Consider the many Old Testament examples, like

Gideon, David, and Ruth. And what about those New Testament heroes, like Peter, Mary Magdalene, and Paul?

And there are many historical and more contemporary heroes of the faith. Take, for example, Fanny Crosby, Brennan Manning, and Abby Johnson, just to name a few.

Perhaps you know such honorable persons—men and women who, with courage, colored the world with valiance in the face of fear. With words, when each knew what was said or written could cost them their lives. With their wisdom, spoken in psalms, songs, and proverbs.

Each of these—every single one—was, or is, broken in some manner. So are you. So am I. Still, we've each been called, no matter what, to honorably color our world—as teachers, physicians, and pastors. As politicians, nurses, and trash collectors, not to mention construction workers, soldiers, speakers, and writers. As moms and dads. Grandparents. Daughters and sons. Siblings. Every one of us—broken crayons—called to color.

One example came to mind recently. I'd taken our daughter, Allie, to school, praying for her and her fellow classmates before arriving on campus. Driving home, I thought about my school days—those seasons of crayons and coloring books, milk and cookies, and, eventually, lockers and lip gloss, as well as blue books and paper-filled three-ring binders.

Once I was home, I turned on the news. The first thing I heard—something my husband had reminded me of prior to leaving for work that morning—was that it was National Dog Day.

The second thing I realized, which brought a surge of sadness, was that it had been exactly one year since thirteen service men and women were killed fighting for freedom. Not their own freedom, but others'. And though it was minor in comparison, many service dogs, faithful canine friends, also lost their lives honorably doing what they were trained to do.

After a few moments, I turned off the television, then sat in silence, pondering those courageous men and women, each broken, no doubt, in some manner of speaking. They sacrificed the comforts of home, risking their lives every day, to color Afghanistan with courage. Which, let's be honest, likely didn't feel much like where they were from. After all, Kabul's not Chicago, Rio Bravo, Sacramento, or tiny Corryton, TN, for example.

Still, each faced the enemy honorably. And it was in that silence—the memory of my early morning commute with Allie as fresh in my mind as the mug of coffee in my hand—when I remembered a particular day thirty-eight years earlier. I remembered a movie my high school English teacher showed our class—the testimony of the honorable Vietnam veteran, David Roever.

And I wondered what the now seventy-seven-year-old Mr. Roever would have to say about the tragedy that occurred those 365 days prior. I'm sure he, like the world, reeled at the news. Because he knows all too well. His life was forever changed when, while serving his country, a phosphorous grenade exploded nearby. Burned beyond recognition, he spent more than a year recovering in the hospital.

Even still, despite extensive physical pain and much emotional and mental suffering as well, he allowed this tragedy to work for triumph. The movie we watched that day in 1985 depicted, with both wit and wisdom, David Roever's reason for joy. Indeed, he shared about the One who was with him in the jungles of Vietnam, and he shared how his Savior, Jesus, has been with him each day since.

Despite being a broken crayon, David Roever is still coloring. And my guess? He'll be doing his best to make the world more beautiful until the Lord calls him home.

What about you? What about me?

As we remember those who lost their lives in Kabul, as we consider all who've fought and sacrificed—many who've died honorably doing so—let's make this our mantra ... our meditation ... our prayer: *Broken crayons still color, so please keep using us, Lord! May You be honored in both our simple and more extraordinary means of service. Amen.*

– 11 –

Honoring Russell

Malcolm Mackinnon

Sometimes I imagine hosting my own Oscars ceremony. But, instead of honoring actors and film-makers, I'd want to celebrate the people who have made a huge impression in my life.

There would, of course, be the obvious winners: Jesus, for securing my salvation; certain Christians who led me to Christ and nurtured my faith; my parents, who brought me up in the way I should go; my wife, for putting up with me; and great friends, for their loyalty.

However, there would also be some unexpected individuals who helped make me what I am today.

One such person is Russell.

I first met Russell at the Art Foundation College weekly disco, when I was seventeen and he was nineteen. The evening was hosted by a fellow student, Martin Martin (yes, that *was* his name), who tried his best to inject some humor into the atmosphere of simmering violence that seemed to accompany all 1980's discos. Aware of the lack of response to his jokes, he tried even harder to make them funny in the misguided belief that everyone would eventually find him hilarious.

And, suddenly, everyone *did* start laughing. Encouraged by the cheers, Martin Martin warmed to his task and told more jokes, relieved that the audience finally understood him.

It took him at least a minute to figure out the people were in fact laughing at Russell and his friend running back and forth across the stage behind him—with no clothes on! Later that evening I was introduced to Russell by a mutual friend. I liked him immediately, especially since he was then finally dressed.

A few weeks later, as my friend and I were about to attend a college workshop, Russell decided he needed to go to a local thrift store and wanted us to join him. Despite the heavy rain, it still sounded like fun. Once inside the store, we tried to find huge sweaters and oversized coats that would reflect our art student image, as well as keep us dry.

A sharp rapping sound interrupted our browsing. We looked at the door, made almost entirely of glass except for the bottom twelve inches, but nobody was there. As we stared, puzzled, a puppet suddenly appeared from below, gesticulating. I laughed insanely, not just at the sight of the puppet dancing around behind the glass, but more because Russell was lying face down on the wet ground keeping out of sight in order to entertain us.

I began to realize Russell was not like anyone else. I came to learn he did nothing for vain reasons, or to show off, or to win anyone's favor. Here was a true creative, an inspirational human, entirely comfortable within his own skin.

My friendship with him grew and I enjoyed being around him. On a weekend trip to a rural art retreat, we struck up a long conversation on the bus taking us there. When all the other students left the bus, taking their belongings with them, Russell turned to me and whispered, "Come on, let's go."

"Don't we need to be in the orientation seminar?" I asked, having not yet reached his level of confident independence.

"No, I've done all this before. You need to be down at the pub with me."

We entered an old rustic inn, one of three in the village. It had four bars, each catering to different groups. Russell took me to the deserted Public Bar. After a few minutes, he rang the bell to let the staff know someone was in the bar. Two minutes later, an old woman appeared, walking slowly. Russell ordered some drinks, the woman served us, and then pottered away to the other bars.

As soon as she left, Russell rang the bell again. She dutifully returned, and he ordered some snacks. After she'd gone, he rang the bell again. She came back and he bought something else.

"Why don't you just order everything in one go, so she doesn't have to keep coming back?" I asked.

"This way, she'll know we need something if the bell rings. If she doesn't hear the bell, she won't come back." The words had barely left his mouth before he had jumped over the bar to pour us both another drink. And another one. And another one. I wanted to protest, but shock and laughter prevented me from doing so.

I'm aware I could be portraying Russell as a criminal or a madman. He was neither. You may be asking how a man capable of streaking and dishonesty could be such an inspiration? But it has less to do with his rule-breaking and more to do with his ability to think and live outside the box.

From a young age, we are encouraged to conform. Expectations are laid out, and guidelines are given to us. To some degree, guidelines are good. They keep us on the right track. They help us follow well-trodden paths to success.

But conventions and codes can also cripple us. They can make us scared to attempt anything innovative, they can stop us thinking for ourselves or exploring the unique personalities God gave each of us.

In the movie *Dead Poets Society*, Robin Williams played a teacher who encouraged his pupils to break free of the stifling expectations that were eliminating their creativity. He urged them to make their lives extraordinary, to suck the marrow out of life, to seize the day, and release their true potential.

Russell lived according to that ethos. He was a character who lit up any room he entered, who gave you a thrill in your heart knowing you could hang out with him for a while. Nobody ever set out on a trajectory of extraordinary living more than him.

Doesn't Jesus encourage us to embrace Him, that we might live lives to the full? His purpose in coming was that we might find life and become the people we were meant to be. That is not to say we turn life into an exercise in self-indulgence, egotism, or crime, but more to dare to live a life of non-conventionality in the same way Jesus did. In doing so, we find our truest identity.

Russell's actions definitely caused me to examine my own life and attitudes. His modest apartment contained a tremendous collection of records, books, clothes, and posters. Visiting him was like entering a modern gallery of all things cool.

One time I knocked on his door and stepped into an apartment containing nothing. And when I say nothing, I mean nothing. Everything had gone.

"Where's all your stuff?"

"I got rid of it."

"What do you mean?"

"I took some stuff to the junk shop, and threw the rest away."

I felt angry. I wanted some of those books. Some of his records were rare and highly sought-after.

"Why did you do that?"

"I wanted to see what it felt like."

"So, what *did* it feel like?" I finally asked, once my annoyance had subsided.

"It felt good. I didn't want my possessions to be in control of me. I wanted to be in control of *them*."

Wow! Talk about being hit between the eyes with a statement. My indignation turned to wonder as I tried to process the thought of waving goodbye to every item I held dear. It sounds like a small thing, but how many people have ever turned their back on their treasured possessions?

I wanted to tell him that normal people just don't do this kind of thing. But, when I thought about it, he obviously had no plans to be normal. And the refusal to do what everyone else did was precisely what made him so extraordinary. Most of all, I envied his strength of mind to rid himself of the trappings of life. Why? Because I realized I *wouldn't* have been able to.

Russell wasn't a Christian. But I've always remembered this occasion, especially when I became a Christian. Here, more than anyone else I've ever known, was a man able to live out the blueprint of Christ that life does not consist in the abundance of our possessions.

I have often wondered what purpose Russell had in my life, considering he never encouraged me in the things of Jesus. But he showed me how to live beyond accepted norms, to think for myself, to grab life by the horns, and, most importantly, to find my true self.

Russell didn't preach about living an exciting life. Instead, he modeled it. He was never rich, never had an amazing job, nor did he constantly travel to exotic places. Yet, he seemed to have made a conscious decision every day to live free from the shackles of other people's expectations.

I haven't seen him for thirty years. I may never see him again. I hope he's alive. I hope he has a faith in Christ. But, for the indelible example he set, and the unforgettable inspiration he gave, I honor him.

– 12 –

Honor With Hope: The Graduation Invitation

Dian Avila

When Daniel turned one, he was already walking and beginning to talk. His older sister, Candace, adored him. She loved helping feed and entertain him. They enjoyed the car ride together to their daycare. Like most working parents, we took turns staying home with the children when they were sick. One Sunday, shortly after Daniel's first birthday, he had a fever and had been crying most of the night. A trip to the doctor gave a diagnosis of an ear infection. Daniel needed to stay home the next day or two. It was my husband, Jose's, turn, since I was still establishing procedures in my fourth-grade class for the new school year.

Meme, Daniel's great-grandmother, screamed for Jose to look at Daniel the next morning as we were getting ready for work. Jose pulled Daniel into his arms, felt him go limp and watched his eyes roll into his sockets. I laid my hand on his head. He was burning up again even with the Tylenol. Jose took Daniel to the doctor, and I went to prepare my classroom for a substitute if needed. When I didn't get a call from Jose right away, I began to relax, believing Daniel was going to be all right. Halfway into our math lesson, someone from the office came into my class, "Your husband is on the phone, I'll take your class."

"Hi, Love. What did the doctor say?"

"Daniel's in the hospital. He has meningitis." Jose's voice cracked.

"I'll be right there."

I rushed to Daniel's hospital crib. He lay tossing and moaning. My hands clutched the cold steel rails. I reached in to pick him up.

"It will hurt him too much to move him. We're giving him pain medication that should start helping soon." The nurse gently pulled my arm away from my baby.

I could hear him grinding his teeth in pain when I leaned in to reassure him that Mommy was with him. That is the memory that haunts me: my one-year-old, laying on his back, looking up into hospital ceiling lights, and gritting his teeth against the pain of meningitis. I put a pacifier in his mouth, even though he had stopped using one at home. He alternately sucked on it and bit down on it. I leaned in again and sang to him. My arms were trembling with the desire to pick him up. The medical team relieved the pain by extracting gelatinous spinal fluid. This was done several times before he rested more comfortably.

Then the waiting began. We waited for the culture to grow and tell us what type of meningitis—pneumococcal. Next, we waited for the antibiotics to fight against it. But during that wait, he had a stroke and had to be rushed by ambulance to Stanford Hospital in Palo Alto. There, they discovered a large stroke, bilateral midbrain infarct, and multiple small brain stem infarcts.

The neurologist's explanation was that Daniel could stay in the quadriplegic state he was in, be severely mentally challenged, just not wake up, or die. Now, the wait was crushing us. And what were we waiting for? The grim options of the neurologist?

Daniel's pediatrician, Dr. Laura Stemmle, came to visit us in the hospital. The neurologist's words still bit us. She had a much better approach. She gave us hope. She made eye contact with me and smiled. "I want an invitation to Daniel's high school graduation." She believed he could make it, and that gave me the hope I needed. We played a song based on Psalm 91 on a tape recorder by his bed. Jose, Jose's mom, and I took turns at his bedside. We sang to him, prayed over him, and talked to him. The days turned into weeks. I spent most of my time at the hospital. Family members brought our daughter, Candace, to visit me. Jose prayed for a sign, just a sign, that he would make it. We both prayed for the strength to endure if he were to die. We continued waiting.

One day when I was returning from a rare trip home to rest, I had trouble keeping my eyes dry enough to see the road. *What if he took a turn for the worse? What if he did wake up and Mommy wasn't there?* It tortured me to be away and my tears were clouding my vision. I moved to the slow lane, preparing to pull over, so I could pull it together. Before I made it to a safe place to park, I felt a presence in the car with me. It wasn't in a single space. It was an encompassing sense that I was not alone. I was surrounded and filled with peace, comfort, and love. My tears stopped and I continued driving. In my heart I knew at that moment Daniel was going to overcome his illness.

Jose was waiting for me at the hospital. He saw that I was excited about something. "What happened?"

"I know Daniel will be ok. I felt as if God told me with His presence that everything is going to be ok." I hugged Jose.

"I'm glad you feel that way, but I don't know. I'm not convinced." He looked back down at our still child.

We prayed together and spent the day beside his crib as we had done for so many days. The next day, we stood in the same spot looking down again with wet eyes on our unmoving boy. "Dian, look! His pinkie moved!"

"What?" I looked where he was pointing and saw for myself. He lifted his pinkie. We yelled for the nurse. The quiet corner of the room was soon a loud flurry of activity. Therapists, nurses, and doctors were coming in. They moved him out of ICU to a room of his own. Candace was able to visit and asked, "Can I hold him?" We gave a resounding "Yes!"

Within a week, he was moved to a rehabilitation hospital. The excruciating wait had come to an end. The next few weeks we watched our son re-learn to walk, eat, grab toys, and mutter sounds.

Daniel did grow up with some learning delays. He didn't start talking until he was five. His reading was delayed as well. But he did graduate from high school, and I remembered to invite Doctors Donald and Laura Stemmle. He also graduated from college and earned a Medical Assisting certificate and an AA degree. The doctors were amazed at how quickly he recovered. But the one doctor I will never forget is the one who gave us hope.

– 13 –

Theology of Honor

Lenette Lindsey

Tears welled up in his eyes, and my tears dropped one by one down my cheeks as I listened to him sing "Auld Lang Syne" for the last time as a graduating senior of the Texas A&M Singing Cadets. Linked arm in arm with the circle of young men, Braedon scanned each face embracing memories made while singing countless songs over the last four years. I caught a slight nod and half smile toward his best friend across the room as they sang, "Should auld acquaintance be forgot and never brought to mind?"

Indeed, many of these friendships may drift apart when the seas distance them, as the song suggests. Yet some will last a lifetime. The memories they have in common are the pillars on which they stood together throughout their service to the Singing Cadets. The same four pillars have been in place for over a century within this collegiate choir: *Purpose, Unity, Spirit, and Honor.*

At Texas A&M, tradition has always been a way of life. Aggies have an undying loyalty to one another and to their school. They call it the Aggie Spirit. Since 1893, they deemed the Singing Cadets the *Voice of Aggieland*. They entertain audiences around Texas, the United States, and even internationally as they represent Texas A&M with their gift of music.

As a parent and former teacher, I can't imagine anything more important than instilling honor in the hearts and minds of our young people. Today's culture often exonerates dishonor for the sake of individualism and freedom. But every Singing Cadet concert and event felt like a Hallmark movie when greeted by young men in formal uniforms with a big smile and a "Howdy, Mrs. Lindsey. It's good to see you." I'd overhear their conversations with each other too, and even then, they spoke with respect, integrity, and kindness.

Braedon told me, "I caught the culture of honor within the Singing Cadets as I watched the older cadets. Then I passed that same culture of honor down to those younger than me." Jakob, the current group's president, agreed.

"I don't think honor is taught. It starts from the top down. Our director, Mr. Kipp, is one of the most honorable men I know. He always helps in times of need, even with the busy agenda of rehearsals. With just a few hours' notice, he transposed the song, 'Oh Love That Wilt Not Let Me Go,' so I could sing it as a solo at my grandfather's funeral."

Men accepted into the Singing Cadets spend their first year in a probationary period. Braedon told me, as a freshman, he was considered a *buffo.* Giggling, I asked, "What's a buffo?"

"It's an Italian word meaning clown of the opera," he said. "It's not hazing, but a year for the buffo to prove themselves by their disciplined work and respect within the group. The experienced Singing Cadets are called Old Men."

This system really works. As respectful as Braedon already was, I noticed even more honorable speech and behavior in his first semester as a cadet. *I'm going to love this group.* When talking to some officers of the Singing Cadets, I learned more about why this model is so successful. Reed, one officer, told me, "Honor is not given; it's earned." But the earning goes both ways between the buffo and the Old Men.

They assign an Old Man to each *buffo* as a mentor. Isaac, the former Singing Cadet president, told me, "We expect Old Men to mentor all the buffo because they look up to them. And as officers, we set the highest example of honor and servant leadership. When standing in line for food, we go last. If anyone is going without, it will be the officers." Indeed, they live out the tradition stated in the handbook: "Old Men should hold themselves to a higher standard than they set for the buffo."[1]

"Sacrificial service is key to who we are and what we do," Jakob said. "Time is our most valuable asset, and we give our time daily." Former President George H. W. Bush chose Texas A&M University for his presidential library and his burial place because he cherished honor. Although he didn't attend the university, he loved their values. "Volunteerism, being one of a thousand points of light, helping others . . . it comes naturally to Aggies," President Bush said.[2]

On a cold, rainy day, December 6, 2018, members of the Singing Cadets and others stood at attention for

---

[1] *Texas A&M Singing Cadets Handbook, 2019-2020*. Singingcadets.tamu.edu. Web. 7 Jun, 2023, p. 51. https://singingcadets.tamu.edu/wp-content/uploads/2019/09/-Handbook-2019-2020.pdf.

[2] Ibid., 46.

about an hour before the presidential train arrived. They greeted President George H. W. Bush home to his final resting place while singing "Mansions of the Lord" as the family exited the train.

The Singing Cadets often sing at funerals. "It's such an honor to give to the families who have lost someone dear to them, even though we may not know them personally," Jakob said. Sadly, in February 2020, the group experienced one funeral they would never forget. Their friend and fellow Singing Cadet, Roel Prado, lost his battle with depression. The Singing Cadets used their gift of music by commissioning a song to honor his life and family. They also created more awareness about depression and those who struggle with it. "What if I Could Tell You," written and composed by Heather Lynn Sorenson, is sung at most of their concerts.

The Singing Cadets taught me a lot about the theology of honor. Even though they are "stellar gentlemen," as Mr. Kipp describes them, they are human, just like you and me. We all have the capacity to show dishonor over honor. And we've done just that by our words and actions. Thankfully, grace and redemption are available daily. Why is honor so important relationally, culturally, and spiritually?

The original Hebrew verb for honor is kâbad (כָּבַד),

meaning "to make honorable."[3] This is the word used in Exodus 20:12 (ESV), *Honor your father and your mother.* Peter uses the Greek equivalent, timaó (τιμάω), meaning "to fix the value" in 1 Peter 2:17a (ESV), *Honor everyone.*[4] If left to our own thinking, we might *fix the value* where we deem it appropriate. But God doesn't tell us only to honor people when they deserve it. He cares about our heart posture—as we bestow honor and when we choose to withhold it. Showing honor creates unity in relationships and fulfills one of the greatest commandments, to love our neighbor as ourselves.

Our society has lost the idea of giving honor where honor is due (Romans 13:7 NIV). Everywhere we turn, people demand honor for themselves in every way possible and withhold it from others. But at each Singing Cadet concert, words of honor are spoken over our military men and women. People recognize and applaud them for their selfless service, and the Singing Cadets sing to honor their sacrifice for the freedom of our country.

---

[3] "H3513 - kāḇaḏ - Strong's Hebrew Lexicon (kjv)." Blue Letter Bible. Web. 15 Jun, 2023. https://www.blueletterbible.org/lexicon/h3513/kjv/wlc/0-1/.

[4] "G5091 - timaō - Strong's Greek Lexicon (kjv)." Blue Letter Bible. Web. 15 Jun, 2023. https://www.blueletterbible.org/lexicon/g5091/kjv/tr/0-1/.

Mr. Kipp states that at the beginning of each concert, they start by praising God, who gave them their voices to sing. They reverently open with a spiritual song, usually an old hymn or a classic like "Ode to Joy" by Beethoven. And at that moment, I think about the words of Psalm 96 (NLT):

> Sing to the Lord; Praise His name. Great is the Lord! He is most worthy of praise! Honor and majesty surround Him; strength and beauty fill His sanctuary. Give to the Lord the glory He deserves.

I've noticed that the Singing Cadets' faces always reflect the mood of the music. They genuinely sing from their hearts about the love of God, love for others, love for our country and the great state of Texas, and of course, Texas A&M University. As seniors, when they circle up and sing "Auld Lang Syne" for the last time, as Braedon did, memories of the countless ways they lived out the verse, "Love one another with brotherly affection. Outdo one another in showing honor (Rom. 12:10 ESV)" will flood their hearts and minds. The Singing Cadets understand the theology of honor.

– 14 –

The Bath

Debra Celovsky

My mother is dying.

Six months after my father's death, she is diagnosed with cancer. Now, just nine weeks after diagnosis, she is receiving hospice care.

Emotionally, the cost has been high. From the moment the call came that Dad was dead by his own hand, life has felt surreal. There is the five-hour trip north to their home, finding Mom surrounded by neighbors, her pastor, and friends. Everyone numb with shock. As my husband embraces her, she leans against him and sobs, "Please pray for me that I won't remember how I found him."

Siblings arrive from other states. We grope for some way of making sense of this unspeakable tragedy. Dad was a pastor much of his adult life. It is the life we grew up in. But depression dogged him. A broken mind or spirit can, like physical trauma, prove unhealing.

In the heat of midsummer in northern California, we work to sort through and clear away the accumulation of fifty-seven years of marriage. It takes two weeks. Mom will live with us after the house is ready for sale. Her grief, which comes in great waves, threatens to drown us all. We do our best to comfort her, our own hearts broken.

In our home, she settles in, quiet, asking for very little, glad to be with us. Mornings she sits on the couch in the living room alcove with her Bible on her lap, reading, praying, sometimes weeping. I feel clumsy and ineffective in my attempts to console her. This is partly due, I know, to my own sorrow in which I seem to be functioning at a distance from reality. A strange mist softens the edges of what happened but, when it clears, I'm left gasping with reality's terrible intensity. It is the same for her, exponentially magnified.

One evening in early December she mentions that she has been a little uncomfortable with a slight swelling in her stomach. I make an appointment right away to see her doctor. He immediately refers her to a specialist. We pray. It takes several weeks for tests, but the diagnosis, when it finally comes, is stage four ovarian cancer.

Our prayers intensify. *She has endured so much, Lord. Have mercy. Please have mercy and heal her.* Yet we know from the hard things already behind us that His will is not always ours, and His will, regardless of the cost in this life, is what we desire.

She opts to fight it. "I think I can win this," she says one day on the way to her weekly appointment with hours of chemotherapy drip. Her voice, with its steady, lifelong faith, is almost more than I can bear in that moment. But her decline is rapid and I finally make the call to hospice.

This is yet more unfamiliar territory. I've heard the stories of hospice care, the abundant generosity accompanying every stage of this difficult passage. The days ahead will prove them true.

One morning the doorbell rings. A lovely young woman stands on the porch holding a plastic container of supplies. Her dark hair is smoothed back in a knot, and she is neatly dressed in a blouse, skirt, and low-heeled shoes. She smiles briefly, her gaze direct, and says, "Hello, my name is Carmen. I'm here from hospice to bathe Mrs. Wheeler." I lead the way to Mom's bedroom, sunlight filtering through the shades and resting on her pale face and quiet form. Carmen greets her in a soft voice and moves to the other side of the bed.

She asks me to fill a shallow pail with water. On the nightstand she sets out a bar of soap, a sponge, a soft cloth, and lotion. Speaking directly to Mom, she says, "I'm going to give you a bath now, so you may just relax." Her movements are practiced and gentle.

After a few moments I can't help but ask, "Have you been doing this long?"

There is a pause. She glances at me with the shadow of a smile. "I lost my sister to cancer, and I do this in her memory."

It takes a moment to absorb what she is saying. *This young woman is bathing my dying mother – and who knows how many others she has served – to honor the memory of a beloved sister.*

There are three of us in that still, sunlit room. My mother, at the end of a life of service to her family and to God's kingdom, soon to be escorted from this life by the Savior she loves. Me, facing another loss, yet recognizing the gifts of grace offered so generously in these last few days. And Carmen, a calm, tender look on her face as she honors a beloved sister while ministering to my own loved one.

The memory of that morning lingers like a benediction, reminding me to esteem and bless those who help ease the journey in this life. And I'm challenged to honor those who've gone on ahead by generously sharing my own gifts of love and tenderness and grace.

– 15 –

The Two Littles

Karen D. Wood

"Mommy is going to come see you soon."

Ellie stared at the phone, then looked up with big, brown eyes filled with tears at her mommy's sister, Aunt Marie, next to her.

One-year-old Kevin bent close to the phone and put his little face on the screen to be as close to his mommy as he could get.

His big sister asked, "When are you coming, Mommy?"

The voice breathed heavily. "Just as soon as I get some money, my babies."

After their mom hung up the phone, Aunt Marie

hugged the two children tightly. She'd promised herself for years that, if it came to it, she'd take good care of them, and she desired to honor that promise to give them a safe home now.

The phone calls were new, as Aunt Marie had recently agreed to take the younger two children, while their mother was in transition. Soon the conflicts with Marie's eldest child, Jack, her twelve-year-old son who, with his extra sensitivities from autism and jealousy, caused drama all day and night. He already had his processing plate full. Transitions were normally difficult, living at both his mom's house and his dad's house, but now his ordered space had been invaded.

"I don't want them here," he yelled.

He crossed his arms and anger flashed in his eyes. "Why don't you take them back to their mommy?"

Inwardly, she flinched, knowing that this transition must be hard on her son, too. "I wish I could, Son. I wish I could." Marie felt so torn.

Jack's attitudes were soon mirrored by the youngest children. Due to broken promises from an absent mommy, the call times became sources of harm and were limited.

This created more confusion and behavior escalations, but there were many things all the children couldn't know, and from which Marie knew she had to protect them. It had been a fifteen-year-old story of her sister being lured into human trafficking, making four babies with four different dads. The oldest brother lived nearby with Marie's mother, Gramma Elaine. An older sister lived with her father hours away and the two littles had been placed with Marie.

As the months passed, the children began to heal. They experienced stability and adjusted to their new surroundings. Previously, while living in the back of a car with their mom for months—finally being rescued during an arrest—food had been limited. At Marie's, the signs of malnutrition diminished, but eating well created constant turmoil.

The littles' attitudes toward food changed almost daily. One day, they'd love a meal, like scrambled eggs. The next day that same meal would cause great tears and refusals. Gramma Elaine and Aunt Marie knew it was about control and comfort, but every meal became exhausting from trying and offering different options.

"No! I don't like it and I won't eat it!" Ellie yelled, throwing the bowl and spraying bits of egg across the table.

Kevin had laid his head on the table, sobbing.

Aunt Marie's chest tightened then softened at such

varied emotions. How could she continue to love these frightened children and still draw the strength she needed each day? Bending close, but not too close, she had gently touched the little girl's tiny shoulder. "Ellie, honey, would you like to—"

"You're not my mommy!" The three-year-old slammed back her head.

Aunt Marie felt the crunch on her nose, another display of the growing hostility from the little girl. She was just old enough to remember the physical violence by inappropriate and unkind men toward her mommy.

"Why do they have to live with us? All they do is scream, and we never go camping anymore!" Jack pushed his chair away from the table and stormed out. She knew it was true. Camping trips couldn't happen now, as the littles had spent too many homeless nights in tents.

The days turned long, the nights became extended energy drains, even with carefully established rituals: dinosaur-print pajamas were chosen, new step stools were pulled up to the bathroom sink, books were chosen from the bookshelf full of story books. The beautiful, antique family heirloom bed that used to be Marie's nightly place of peace was now occupied with children. The same songs were sung, "This Little

Light of Mine," "Jesus Loves the Little Children," and "Twinkle, Twinkle, Little Star."

Marie tried to create as much laughter, hugs, and kisses as she could, tucking the littles into bed with their favorite plush animals and blankies. Then, she tiptoed out of the silent room. But immediately, Ellie would start to cry and scream and thrash around. "You are not my mom! I want my mommy!"

Lying in bed, Kevin stared blankly at the ceiling, not making a sound.

* * *

Marie sat in the courthouse waiting room, anticipating yet another morning of wondering when the call would come for her to enter the courtroom. Her sister, the mother of the children, had fled to another state with the man who had abused her. She appeared by teleconference at so many of the hearings, and finally the judge had enough of the excuses, and decreed the two little were to proceed to adoption with Marie.

Now, she looked over the adoption paperwork. Questions flooded her mind. Was it fair to her son to invade his ordered space and disrupt his life? If she couldn't keep these kids, who could? These precious littles already had so much stacked against them. What would happen to them?

It wasn't just their abandonment they would process as they grew. Marie looked down at the book in her bag, *The Deepest Well,* which had introduced her to the concept of childhood trauma impacting health into adulthood. She had taken the trauma survey mentioned in the book, Adverse Childhood Experiences (ACEs), knowing a score of three or four was considered high risk. As she scored the survey for the littles, she had chills as she realized each had scored a ten out of ten. That number was adding to the weight of the decisions she was making for their future. Yet she had read that one person could make a difference in the healing process. Would that be her?

She returned home, and she heard a rustle in the doorway. Jack was waiting for her.

"Mom, why do we have to be the new home? Why don't we go camping anymore?"

Realizing this was a critical moment, she said, "Honey, I know having new people in the house is hard for you. We've had so many years together, and now it is time to share our love with children who need a home."

He shuffled his feet on the carpet. "Please can just you and I go camping like we used to?"

* * *

The sun lowered in the sky. The brilliant, peaking colors glimmered between open spaces of the redwoods.

The water came to boil in the pan. Marie pulled two mugs out of the camping boxes and filled them with hot water. "Water's ready!"

"I'll get the hot chocolate!" He opened the box. "You got the kind with marshmallows! You're the best mom!"

They sat cozy by the fire, wrapped in a blanket together.

He poked at the marshmallows. "Do you think Ellie and Kevin would like hot chocolate when we get back?"

"They'd love it. What do you think?"

He looked down and thought before speaking. "I think so, too."

* * *

As time passed, the two littles began to talk more, better able to communicate their needs and feelings. They loved their teachers and flourished in preschool. Graduation heralded a big celebration of great things to come.

Jack tugged his mom's sleeve. "Mom, look at Ellie!"

Dressed in her yellow robe and graduation hat, Ellie waved as she stood so proudly on the stage holding her diploma. Later she said, "Look what I got!"

"It's beautiful, darling. We are so proud of you!" Aunt "Mom" Marie smiled, tears in her eyes.

The graduation pictures were added to the family wall of photos: three smiling children.

* * *

Toys, chickens, a playset, and a garden—all for the littles—now filled the large backyard. On the back steps were an array of adult-sized boots, medium-sized boots, and two sets of little boots.

Ellie put her boots on and followed Marie around the garden with the miniature wheelbarrow and shovel. "What goes in this hole?"

"Squash, so you and Jack and Kevin can grow big and strong." Marie placed a few seeds into Ellie's palm.

"Mom, look!" Jack shouted from the playset. "I helped Kevin go down the slide!"

"Good job, boys!" Marie said, laughing as she nodded at Ellie, who ever so gently dropped the seeds into the hole.

"Would you like to cover the hole, or do you want me to do it?"

"I can do it all by myself." Ellie scooted the dirt over the hole.

"You did it!"

Ellie's smile brightened, as she said, "Thanks, Mom."

– 16 –

Hero (for Victor)

Christine Hagion

No one cheered for you
or the other soldiers who survived the jungle horrors…
When your injured foot stepped onto American soil,
you faced a more insidious enemy:
not the foreign faces of the Viet Cong.
But the familiar ones: neighbor, classmate.
Friend.
Those who knew you,

yet now reviled you
because you wore the uniform.
Because you fought the war that could not be won
despite our military might,
due to lack of vision
and uncompromising resolve.

You were used as pawns
in our political games.
Your sweat, your blood
flowed in rivers of intrigue and betrayal…
Your torture and terror
lost in antipathy as we sat
from our comfortable chairs, our cozy living rooms.
We watched you tremble
from the driving fear and the dripping rain,
as the faceless soldier stared back at us
from the flickering screens of our electronic
conscience.

I cannot imagine the terrors you faced,
the friends you lost,
the taste of blood; the stench of death,
the ripping of your flesh by your tormentors,
the fear that pierced through to the soul.

Sometimes in your sleep, I know
you still hear the choppers.
But I wonder
  do you hear the cheering?
The silent whoops and hollers,
the marching bands playing
  celebrating your safe return,
your incredible and hard-won victory?

Instead of seeing bodies,
do you see the balloons
and the ticker-tape parade
  in your honor

that take place every time I see your face,
or your scarred back,
or touch your wounded soul
that you guard so fiercely?

For your bravery did not end the day
that you took off that uniform.
Nor did your war.
I see your courage every day.
As you fight for principle,
as you stand for honesty,
for integrity, for justice.
I see you bravely face discrimination
and combat discouragement.
As you marched boldly to the front,
so you push onward today
to an uncertain future,
armed with nothing more
than self-confidence and perseverance.

For this, you are to be commended
    with a medal that cannot rust or corrupt.
        For valor uncommon,
awarded by those whose hearts
    you have captured
      with love, in respect,
            and honor.

– 17 –

Honoring the Pieces of Your Heart

Darcy Schock

Great, I have to do life with you again today. It was the first thought that entered my mind after the chipper chorus of the alarm stirred me awake. I pressed *snooze* and clamped my eyes shut against the hot prickle of tears.

The black, soundless morning pushed heavy on my heart. Heavier than the piles of blankets on top of me. No birds chirped their cheerful melody to welcome me into the new day. Not in the dead of winter. The warm glow from the sun wouldn't break for at least a half-hour.

I lay in the darkness, longing for the peace of sleep.

My only reprieve from the condemning thoughts that taunted my days.

It's a hopeless feeling being trapped with a person you don't like. It's even worse when the person is you.

That morning was the first moment I realized how much self-hate had infiltrated my life. I knew I needed to make some major changes. I started by asking myself, *How did I get here and how do I leave?*

As the months unfolded, I slowed my life down so I could process the inner turmoil. I read many books and I attended counseling sessions.

The deeper into it I got, the more I realized there was a hurting child inside. As I processed my childhood, a fuzzy movie reel unfolded in my mind.

A bleach-blonde pig-tailed girl trots on the scene. She is radiant and free. She loves exploring and dreams up story after story while making trips to the library.

I looked at that girl with excitement for all the pieces that form the beauty inside her heart. Her unique traits shined with hope. I marveled at the way God created her.

But then other images splayed across the screen. The same girl, with a sparkle in her eye, stared up at an adult.

"What do you want to be when you grow up?" the

important-looking lady asked.

"I want to be a librarian," the pig-tailed girl replied.

The adult adjusted her purse strap and says, "Well, that won't take you anywhere in life."

The little girl's gaze dropped to her scuffed tennis shoes, and she kicked at a rock. What she heard was, *the passions in your heart are not good enough.* As an onlooker, I saw the sparkle dim. A cloud of doubt replaced it.

As I continued to watch this movie from my past, I saw multiple instances like this. I realized something. As the opinions of others cut into my heart, doubts seeped in. Somewhere amidst the cadence of life, I lost honor toward the pieces of my heart. I stopped believing in the unique way God created me and the things that made my heart sing.

With each careless opinion, the wild and free young girl with a sensitive heart had broken off another God-ordained piece. Over time, she put those pieces in a dark box, closed the cover, and slapped on a label that read: *Bad stuff. Keep out.*

Instead of doing the things written on her heart by her Creator, she poured herself into doing what she thought others wanted. She became eloquent at saying what others wanted to hear and doing what they wanted her to do. And for a time, it seemed to work.

Until she woke up that dark morning and realized she hated herself.

She hated who she had become because it wasn't who she was created to be. But she didn't feel she could be herself . . . because, in the past, it hadn't been good enough.

In one of my lowest moments, God brought a Bible verse to mind:

> He also brought me out into a broad place; He delivered me because He delighted in me (Psalm 18:19 NKJV).

The thought that anyone would *delight* in me was foreign for the longest time. My negative experiences with people had blinded me from the love I currently had—from God and others—while also keeping me in a prison of fear. I was living life with a mask, too afraid to be vulnerable.

With God's gentle promptings, and the patient, safe people He blessed me with, I found the courage to crack open that dusty box. With trembling hands, I pulled out a few of my heart's broken pieces. The more pieces I pulled out and allowed God to heal, the more freedom and courage I found. Slowly, God restored the person He created me to be.

I realized the way I had been living was a frantic attempt to please everyone. I had wrongly believed that what people thought about me translated into what God thought about me. And if I just did enough good things and pleased enough people, I would be good enough.

But that isn't the truth of God's Word. Yes, we're called to honor others. Yes, we're called to honor God. But that honor isn't heartfelt if it's planted in fear, or in a desire to measure up.

God really laid on my heart that I couldn't honor and value others if I couldn't honor myself. Jesus Himself says, '*You shall love your neighbor as yourself*' (Mark 12:31 NKJV). What does love for others look like if we are simmering in self-hate?

None of us escape this life without wounds or broken pieces. But none of us are purposeless either. Our pain and failures don't define us. God's love does.

God created your heart with intention, and He chose you. You are royalty. A son or daughter of the King. I don't know what lies have been spoken over you. Or what experiences have tempted you to believe you're more trash than beauty, but I can tell you about the power of believing the truth of what God says about you. I understand the struggle to rise above lies. But I can also tell you it's worth it.

The kingdom of God is far more beautiful and

incomprehensible than we can wrap our finite minds around. You have a place in His kingdom, and the pieces of your heart play a role.

As you embark on this important mission of learning how to honor the pieces of your heart, I have found a few weapons to be helpful. Foremost, time in the Word and in prayer, but beyond that, here are a few other helpful ideas.

Find truth-tellers. We all know the truth in our mind. But it can be life changing when we surround ourselves with safe people who see our value and can tell us the truth again and again, without getting annoyed. Relationships hold power to help us move the truth from our minds into our hearts.

Take time to do things that bring you peace and joy. For so long, this felt selfish to me. Why should I do something for myself when there is so much to do for others? Because we can't give what we don't have. If we are empty and filled with self-hate, that spirit pours out no matter how big of a smile we plaster on our face. It's not selfish to find time to fill up your soul. Whether it's from reading, sewing, baking, gardening, hiking, painting, etc. If you don't know what you love, try out different things until you discover that sweet spot.

Receive God's love. What would you do if you lived

as if you were loved? Would you be braver? Have more courage to act upon the things God places on your heart? Would you reach out in vulnerability to the people God nudges you toward? When we live as if we're loved (because we are!) fear can't hold us back.

Search your heart for any moments of pain from your childhood you may not have addressed. Maybe you brushed it off as not that bad. If hurt still lingers, have compassion on that part of yourself. It's okay. Take a moment to say sorry to that young child.

Don't negate counseling. You are worth the time and money it takes to help you find a healthy view of yourself.

If any of that resonated with you, I want to hand you some hope. Dawn is coming. It's time to push the covers back, open the shades, and stand in the radiant truth that you are crowned with glory and honor. I encourage you to lift your chin up and declare that honoring the precious pieces of your heart is worth it.

– 18 –

Three Keys for Honoring Father and Mother

A Devotional Exploration for 21st Century Christians

Terrie Hellard-Brown

If you honor your father and mother, 'things will go well for you, and you will have a long life on the earth' (Eph. 6:3 NLT).

A Taiwanese friend who had recently become a Christian asked, "If I write a message to my dad on a T-shirt and burn it for him, can I tell him how I feel?" She wanted so badly to share her love and respect with her recently deceased father. Another young man told me he could not become a Christian until after he fulfilled his responsibilities to his father as the oldest son. He struggled between his desire to follow Christ and the knowledge that his family would not understand if he did not honor his father into the afterlife.

Most Asian cultures teach that honoring parents goes beyond this life. In Taiwan, when parents die, the oldest child specially honors them by caring for them in the afterlife until they are later reincarnated. Ancestor worship is often part of family life. The traditional religion teaches people to burn ghost money and pictures of whatever their loved one needs in the afterlife. Many pray to their deceased relatives. Honoring father and mother in these ways requires far more than what the Bible teaches, and the Christian understanding of honor.

On the other hand, once when my husband preached a sermon about honoring one's parents, he was accosted after the service by a woman who had been abused. "You cannot tell people to honor their fathers and mothers when they've lived with a father who has abused them!" Recently, another young woman asked about the same thing when taught she needed to forgive: "But what if your mother betrayed and abused you? I can't forgive her."

If we've grown up in a Christian environment, then we've heard all our lives, "Honor your father and mother." With the promise attached to it for long life, we may really want to master this one. Personally, however, I wasn't sure what it meant to honor my father and mother. And did the long life just mean that; because I listened to them and didn't run out in the street, I lived longer than I would have if I'd ignored their warnings? Or was there more to this whole thing?

In Taiwan's culture, honoring parents can mean the difference between life and death. A child may be disowned or shamed so that the child becomes suicidal. We've ministered to many who were on the edge of despair simply because they did something to dishonor their parents. In the ancient Jewish culture, dishonor could literally lead to death. God's Law said, *Anyone who dishonors father or mother must be put to death. Such a person is guilty of a capital offense* (Leviticus 20:9 NLT). So, does this promise still apply in our culture where we do not typically disown a disrespectful child, and we do not kill them?

From what I've seen, in the American culture, to honor our parents seems to mean obeying them or submitting to their wishes while we are children. Once we're adults, in many cases, we are on our own, making life decisions without much consideration of our parents' wishes. Or the parents' wishes, though considered, often do not change a child's plans. Our Western culture is more individualistic in nature. Taiwan's culture is more familial where children will obey their parents even into marriage and adulthood.

Living in these two cultures caused me to explore these scriptures more deeply. I had questions like: Does honoring simply mean obeying parents while we are children? Does it go into adult years? When does honoring become worship? How can I honor my parents and still follow God when the two disagree?

We find clarification in Scripture: *Honor (respect, obey, care for) your father and your mother, so that your days may be prolonged in the land the LORD your God gives you* (Exodus 20:12 AMP). So, if we begin by defining honor in this way, we have a foundation.

Respect

This is the biggest part of honoring our parents. We need to respect them because they are our parents, and hopefully, because of all they have done for us. However, we know some parents do not live up to their role. They abuse, criticize, and hurt their children, or they don't provide for basic needs or withhold affection and love. As a child of such parents, one can still show respect because of the office of parent. We naturally want to respect our parents even when their imperfections are at the forefront.

The scriptures that guide our hearts, minds, and attitudes for showing respect are:

> Honor [esteem, value as precious] your father and your mother [and be respectful to

> them]—this is the first commandment with a promise—so that it may be well with you, and that you may have a long life on the earth (Eph. 6:2-3 AMP).

> My son, obey your father's commands, and don't neglect your mother's instruction (Prov. 6:20 NLT).

If we've had to deal with abuse or betrayal from a parent, James 5:16 can guide us. Our prayers and forgiveness can make so much difference in our own hearts and in our relationships.

> Confess your sins to each other and pray for each other so that you may be healed. The earnest prayer of a righteous person has great power and produces wonderful results (James 5:16 NLT).

This verse works in relationships. A father betrayed his family by having several affairs, and the marriage ended in divorce after over twenty years of marriage. The daughter felt betrayed and hurt by the way the father treated her throughout her childhood. She found it difficult to show respect to a man who never showed love or respect to her. However, God convicted her that she needed to pray daily for her dad, and she needed to pray for God to bless him. God worked on her heart bringing healing and wholeness to her as He reaffirmed that He was her perfect Father. Then, a miracle happened in her relationship with her dad. Letting go of expectations, she could forgive and build a relationship with him. She could show respect to him just because he was the dad who gave her life. And then, God did an even bigger miracle when He changed her dad's heart. Today, this father and daughter have a good relationship, and her father is following God with all his heart. "His prayers are like a sermon. His humility and love for God are real. I love my dad, and I'm so grateful God is truly our Redeemer," she said.

Obey

As we look at the Scriptures, God seems to be directing His command to obey parents to children, not adults. We're instructed not to forget what our parents taught us, but we don't seem to have the same command to obey our parents as adults.

> Children, obey your parents because you belong to the Lord, for this is the right thing to do. Fathers, do not provoke your children to anger by the way you treat them. Rather, bring them up with the discipline and instruction that comes from the Lord (Eph. 6:1, 4 NLT).

These verses say "bring them up," clearly indicating raising children.

Care For

This is the part that applies to honoring our parents when we are adults. Several verses make it clear that we are to care for our parents in their old age.

> For instance, Moses gave you this law from God: 'Honor your father and mother,' and 'Anyone who speaks disrespectfully of father or mother must be put to death.' But you say it is all right for people to say to their parents, 'Sorry, I can't help you. For I have vowed to give to God what I would have given to you.' In this way, you let them disregard their needy parents. And so you cancel the word of God in order to hand down your own tradition. (Mark 7:10-13 NLT).

These verses and others clearly teach that we have a responsibility to honor our parents in their old age by providing for them as needed. We cannot use the excuse that we have dedicated our resources to God to neglect our parents. This does not honor them or God.

So, according to God's Word, we are to honor our parents as children by obeying them, as adults by caring for them, and throughout our lives by showing them respect. Honoring our parents should never become worship. Our worship is for God alone. However, we can honor God as we honor our parents in the correct, biblical ways.

– 19 –

Glorify With Gratitude

Dian Avila

I stared through the giant screened window that made up the southern wall of our bedroom. No hibiscus leaves or palm fronds swayed. No smells drifted in from the large, green compound. Even the birds' chirping sounded sedated. *Lord, I'm in this sweltering jungle for you. Why have you not healed me? How many more weeks or months must I cry out to you before I feel any relief?*

A moan slipped past my parched lips as tears and sweat mingled. My husband, Jose, came in and saw my tears. He picked up my hand as he sat beside me. "Jose, I'm so tired and sore. I don't understand." His kiss felt cool on my forehead. He prayed with me, again.

I must have dozed because I heard the evening's cicadas, bats, and frogs. I pushed myself up, turned on the light, and opened my treasured Bible. *We are hard pressed on every side, but not crushed; perplexed but not in despair; persecuted, but not abandoned; struck down, but not destroyed* (2 Cor. 1:7 NIV). Tears spilled onto my cheeks. The warmth of the Lord's love replaced the heat of the rain forest. I had so much to be thankful for. I was not being persecuted, struck down, or abandoned. I realized that evening in my room in Pucallpa, Peru, that the only thing that needed healing was my attitude. I resolved to stop focusing on the pain and begin praising God and counting my multiple blessings.

When had I stopped doing that? I believe it was when my disease first flared up. I prayed with the expectation of a quick recovery. When it didn't come, I began to despair. In our five years as missionaries, we had seen so many miracles from our adoring Lord. But this time, *He* saw the wisdom of delaying His healing hand. His timing is always perfect.

Healing did not come for many more weeks after my epiphany, but I spent those weeks appreciating every blessing instead of focusing on my illness. I embraced His love. I replaced thoughts of pity with remembrances of the truth of Jesus. In ways none of us could have orchestrated without God, I did find healing two weeks before we returned to the States.

We rightly think of honoring God with obedience and praise. But glorifying God also includes accepting with gratitude everything He allows in our lives. Even when it seems like a sacrifice to give Him thanks. *Sacrifice thank offerings to God, fulfill your vows to the Most High* (Ps. 50:14 NIV). Experiencing God is the most important blessing any of us can enjoy. So, whatever circumstances bring us to truly embrace His love, we can truly be thankful for them. How are you glorifying God with your gratitude today?

– 20 –

An Honored Disciple

Kelly Conley

'Well done, good and faithful servant! You have been faithful with a few things; I will put you in charge of many things' (Matthew 25:21 NLT).

Jesus honors us with abundant blessings, even with the struggles we face in the world—like difficult relationships, addictions, or challenging leadership roles. If we are spending our time, talents, and money on the Kingdom of God, we will face greater warfare—the battle of Satan for our souls. Perhaps you are facing the pain of loss, overcome with fear and worry, or hurt by past abuses. In these times of warfare, it would seem that God is not paying attention to what is happening in our lives, or that He is not protecting us when we are experiencing trouble.

Yet the opposite is true.

As Jesus puts us in charge of more things, we can rest assured that He is right beside us. Jesus says, *'I have told you these things, so that in me you may have peace. In this world, you will have trouble. But take heart! I have overcome the world'* (John 16:33 NLT). You may face trouble with each increased responsibility, but your soul will be at peace when you honor Jesus with your obedience.

During my early twenties, my soul was weary and my heart heavy. I lived a life of poverty, unable to embrace adulthood. I drank, could not hold down a job, and failed to build healthy relationships. When I got sober, I lived peacefully for a while, making ends meet, and attending Alcoholics Anonymous. Even though I had become better equipped, I felt as though my life was on hold and my purpose empty. Eventually, I discovered a workshop for Christians in recovery. As I participated in the group, I began to experience the hope that comes when Jesus Christ is knocking at the door to my heart.

After receiving Christ, I was blessed with peace and purity in my soul beyond anything I had imagined. Year after year studying the Word of God, I have learned to connect with others and serve others in God's Kingdom. God has increased my responsibilities tenfold, which has brought me the cherished joy and peace I had desired.

When our obedience to Jesus increases, we become responsible for more things. God honors us by all He has given us. And even when the world's troubles threaten to overwhelm us, He equips us to handle more responsibility according to His will, so that we will be able to walk as His faithful servants.

Dear Jesus: You have honored Your precious daughter with a purpose, responsibility, and promise that, whilst I am obedient to Your call, I will experience peace in my heart knowing that You are always beside me. In Jesus' Name, Amen.

– 21 –

First Things First

Kimberly Novak

I sank into a chair in my grandparents' sunroom, exhausted and sweaty. Time spent in the garden with Dad was hard work, and I looked forward to a rest. As I settled in, I realized I hadn't been in that room since Gramps died. Suddenly, relaxation was no longer a priority. I rose to get reacquainted, allowing my fingers to glide across the unfinished puzzle on the table. A bookshelf on the opposite wall held all of Gramp's favorite titles. Next to his Bible was a jar of buttons. I reached up to grab the jar when Dad entered the room.

"Hey, Lucas, you know house rules. You better get

cleaned up before anyone catches you slopping up the floor."

Intrigued about the jar, I ignored that I was filthy. "What's with the jar of buttons?"

"Mom and I found it when we were cleaning the attic yesterday. I thought they were lost when Gramps passed away."

I remember spending time here when Gramps was sick, but was sure that I never saw that jar. "Was it always in the sunroom?"

"Gramps kept the jar alongside his Bible, but the location always changed. Let's grab a seat outside. No one will be happy if we mess up this room more than you already have. I'll explain the buttons on the porch."

"First things first," we said before leaving the sunroom. No matter the circumstance, Gramps always began with the phrase *first things first.* He followed by opening his Bible and reading a passage aloud. We both knew what to do next. Dad headed for the stoop with the jar, and I retrieved the Bible.

"Go ahead, son, you choose the passage."

Dad cradled the jar, and I held the Bible gently to avoid disturbing how Gramps left it and turned to his favorite verse. *I give thanks to you, O Lord my God, with my whole heart, and I will glorify Your name forever*

(Psalm 86:12 NRSV). Reading the verse connected me to Gramps and, for that, I was grateful. I gently set the Bible down and Dad handed me the container.

"Open it, but do it carefully."

I poured a few buttons into my hand. They were shiny, flat, and of different shapes and sizes. "Okay, Dad, spill it. I can tell you have a story to tell."

Taking the jar from my hands, Dad poured a handful of buttons into his palm and held them tightly. "No matter what we were doing, where we were going, or who was involved, Gramps had a way of turning the ordinary into an extraordinary faith-filled moment. I was about your age when he asked me to help with the gardening, and my adolescent response met his request with a grunt."

I knew what he meant. I grumbled a time or two about the same task, but never imagined Dad reacting that way.

"Gramps was hard-working and tough on the exterior, but there was also a sensitive God-loving side that he allowed me to see when a situation was teachable in his eyes."

Teachable like the moment we are in now, I thought. I adjusted my posture, took a sip of soda, and listened eagerly.

"The best day, which will always be in my heart,

was when he surprised me with matching overalls."

I wanted to laugh, but it served no purpose since we sat side by side in identical overalls. "Gardening needs to be better. Why do we have to look like Farmer Ted?"

"Trust me. As you get older, what once seemed unimportant will become meaningful."

And there it was, Dad's opening for the life lesson he was about to thrust upon my young mind. I was happy at how much he reminded me of Gramps, and I felt I was paying him homage by showing my interest.

"Let's run down what we know so far. We sit in twin overalls like you and Gramps once sat. You were not a fan of gardening, but you did it anyway. Where do the buttons fit in?"

Dad giggled at my inquisition. "Initially, I whined about gardening almost as much as you do. Soon, though, it became fun and something I wanted to do daily."

I looked at him as a teenager should, perplexed at the thought, but curious as to how it might be something I would enjoy in the future.

"Your grandparents were wonderful and instilled the virtues of faith, hope, and love in our family. I hope your mom and I have passed that along to you. Gramps took every opportunity to combine his work with prayer and, even in my youth, I could see how much he loved God as he worked in the garden and I became a kid on a mission."

Hearing those words brought memories to mind of seeing Gramps work in the garden. His demeanor was always pleasant and carefree.

"I mirrored every move he made, trying to learn as much as possible about gardening and doing God's work. It wasn't long before I adopted the *first things first* attitude."

The thought of the two of them warmed my heart and also made me laugh. "I can just picture you walking toe to toe in these ridiculous overalls."

Dad gave me a sly smile. "One day, Gramps had me working on a pile of broken and wilted branches. My instruction was to plant them on the back edge of the garden. He had this grand idea to honor God by faithfully believing they would sprout with new life."

His gaze turned away from mine, and I could sense his need to hold back tears as I struggled to do the same.

"It had been a long day. I was exhausted and worked carelessly. I grabbed hold of the longest branch and, as I shoved it into the ground, the top of the branch caught my shoulder strap, forcing a button clear off."

"Is it safe to say that he fixed your strap with one from this jar?"

"Eventually, but in this first instance, he dislodged one of his own, said a prayer, and placed it in the ground. As time passed, this became a regular event, and I would need a new fastener almost every time we were in the garden. Gramps would fetch what he called his jar of "faithful replacements" and fix me up. The blue one I dislodged while removing a hungry rabbit from the strawberry patch. Gramps put the big gold one on in its place. Every button in this jar holds a prayer and a story."

"If this was a regular occurrence, why have we not found any of the buttons all the time we have worked in this garden?"

"Behind the scenes, Gramps would go ahead of me early each morning, retrieve what we buried, and place them in this jar. It's also a safe bet that your grandmother had her role in making sure there were always enough."

"He was using recycled buttons and you fell for it!" It was fantastic to learn that Gramps had a sense of humor similar to mine and that he and Grandma were in cahoots!

"Yes, eventually I caught on, but it didn't make a difference. What mattered to me were the conversations, laughs, and memories."

I was eager to hear more when I remembered the

dried-up twigs. "Can we circle back to the fact that Gramps had you plant lifeless branches?"

"Ha! Yes. I continued watering and caring for the branches, including the surrounding dirt. After about two weeks, we saw new growth. I later learned that Gramps planted tiny seeds deep in the ground."

The lengths Gramps went to instill virtues of honor and faith in God meant a lot to Dad, and he passed that on to me. But there was still a missing piece. "What did Gramps do with the old sticks when the new plants grew?"

"What's the first gardening tool I taught you to use?"

"The woodchipper!"

"I learned on that very one! Gramps and I would load the twigs and use the fresh mulch in the garden beds."

I became motivated by Dad keeping the memory of Gramps alive and decided to make something special out of the day. Tugging at my strap until the button came free, I handed it to him.

"What's this?"

"It's my way of celebrating Gramps and his memory. Let's plant something to last for generations."

– 22 –

A Brown Sugar Box from Home

Debbie Jones Warren

For five years I've been writing short stories about my childhood in a boarding school in Nigeria. Most of these vignettes are melancholy because I'm searching to find where God was during the ten years I lived away from home beginning at age six. My mom listens to my stories, together we shed a few tears, then she encourages me to keep writing. As I'm healing from the trauma, happy memories are emerging. I share this story to honor my 91-year-old mother for her many sacrifices during her thirty years on the mission field.

Dad ran a hand over his stubbled chin as he stepped into the kitchen of our mission home in Nigeria. "Marcy, there's a plane coming tomorrow. Do you have any snacks to send to Kent Academy for Larry and Debbie?"

Mom dried her hands on the apron covering her yellow, knee-length cotton dress. "Oh, no." She crinkled her forehead. "We ate the last of the sugar cookies with our afternoon tea."

Dad patted Mom's back and sighed. "I'm sorry I didn't tell you about the plane earlier. I've been preparing for tomorrow's geometry class to stay ahead of my Nigerian high school students."

The weary woman turned and slipped her arms around the waist of Dad's tall, slender frame. "I've just finished washing the dinner dishes, but I could still bake a batch of cookies."

Dad grinned. "It's 7:30 p.m., so you have two hours before the station's generator shuts down for the night. If anyone can do it, you can."

"You're right!. But you'll have to put our three little ones to bed." Mom pulled a mixing bowl from the cupboard. "I asked Mark and Grant to play nicely with baby Cindy until I was finished here."

She opened the oven, turned the gauge, and bent to light the flame with the metal starter wand. "Once the cookies are baking, I'll write a letter to our second-and third-grade kids at K.A." She paused and looked up at Dad with tears in her eyes. "I miss them while they're at school. I wish they could stay with us and study at home somehow."

Dad rubbed his eyes. "I miss them, too. But we know the school is the best place for them. Thanks for doing this baking on such short notice." He stepped toward the doorway, then stopped and frowned. "Do we have enough flour and sugar? We haven't been to Ilorin for a few weeks to shop."

Mom nodded. "We still have plenty in the storeroom."

You're such a whiz in the kitchen." Dad's eyes twinkled. "You can whip up anything from nothing!"

Mom brushed a short, dark strand of hair from her face. "Fortunately, I bought more milk from the Fulani herdsman who stopped by yesterday, so I'll make sugar cookies again. Remember how Debbie calls them *Fulani cookies*?"

"Yes, and we all love your Fulani cookies." Dad patted his stomach as he headed toward the living room.

Mom measured the ingredients, stirred the batter, and soon two trays of tasty treats were in the oven. Then she scooped batter onto the two remaining pans.

Once the cookies were cooling, Mom sat at the dining room table. She slipped a sheet of carbon paper under the first page of a notepad so she could write two letters at once. Then she jotted down the family activities of the past week.

The letter ended with, "That's all for now. Lots of love, Mom and Dad, Mark, Grant, and Cindy."

In the kitchen, she opened a lower cabinet door and rummaged through empty boxes. "Here they are!" She pulled out two brown sugar boxes she had saved just for this purpose and lined them with waxed paper. Carefully placing one cookie after another in neat rows, she wedged as many as she could into each carton.

Dad pressed tape on the packages as Mom held the wrapping in place. "I can picture our kids' smiles when these arrive."

"Larry and Debbie will be excited to get packages!" Mom hugged them to her chest then used the hem of her apron to wipe a tear from her cheek. "I wish we could deliver these in person."

* * *

The midday sun shone brightly as my roommate and I ran across the playground toward the boarding school dining hall, our arms straight out to the sides. Veering left, then right, then left again, we soared and dipped over the asphalt like airplanes. Suddenly the hum of an engine buzzed overhead. We stopped and looked at the sky, holding our hands over our eyes to shield them from the sun.

"I wonder where that plane is coming from." I waved toward the sky.

"Maybe it's bringing us mail from home!" My friend's voice squeaked high as she flew in a circle around me.

After lunch I raced to the girls' dorm. There, we second graders brushed our teeth and settled carefully onto our neatly made beds for a short rest before afternoon classes.

Soon an auntie walked down the hall, stopping from room to room and handing out the day's mail. "Here are letters for two of the girls in this room."

All four of us looked up.

She stood by my bed and smiled. "One's for you, Debbie. And you also have a package."

I hugged the brick-shaped parcel as if I were hugging Mom. Butterflies danced in my tummy as I tried to guess the treat inside. First, I opened the letter and read the news about Mark, Grant, and Cindy. How lucky they were to still live at home.

I took my time opening the brown package. *Look how carefully Mommy placed the tape. I love her handwriting. I don't want to rip anything.*

Finally, I spread the paper open. There sat a brown sugar box.

One of my roommates asked, "Why did your mom

send you sugar?"

I laughed. "I think she just used the box." Sure enough, inside were cookies—Fulani cookies. I took one out and sniffed. The smell of sugar and vanilla tickled my nose.

I bit into the soft mound. Instantly, I was back home on our village mission station helping Mom stir the dough . . . taking fingerfuls of batter . . . handing the spoon for Larry to lick. I sure missed home.

The girl in the lower bunk across from me opened her package of roasted peanuts and held it out to me.

"Want some?"

I wanted to taste the peanuts. But I couldn't bear to give up a single bite of Fulani cookies.

"No thanks," I said.

From the bunk above me, my roommate leaned over the railing. "Hey, Debbie. What is it your mom sent you this time?" Her parents lived in Dahomey, a neighboring country, and she didn't get many letters. Her eyes drooped.

"These are cookies made with milk from Fulani cows, plus lots of flour and sugar." I felt bad she never got packages. We were both homesick. Maybe a cookie would help her feel better.

I handed one up to her.

"Thank you!" Her face broke into a grin and she

took a nibble. "Mmmm. So sweet and sugary."

Mom would be proud that I shared her cookies.

After a while, the auntie came down the hall and collected our goodies. "I'll put these in a tin in the cookie cupboard. They'll be in the office next to the girls' lobby, and you can eat from yours each afternoon until you finish them."

After rest hour, as I walked to school, I saw my brother and waved. "Hi, Larry! Did you get a package from home?"

"Yes, I did. Fulani cookies! They were so good." He smacked his lips together. "I ate half of them already."

"Some kids never get anything," I said. "We're lucky Mom and Dad send us a letter *and* tasty cookies really often."

Over the next week, I took two cookies from the brown sugar box every rest hour. I imagined having teatime with Mom as she and I sat at the kids' table on our porch.

The day I ate the last cookie in my bed, I faced the wall, curled up like a cat, and nibbled in secret. While I bit off teeny, tiny pieces savoring the love from my mom, my heart felt as heavy as a rock.

After rest hour, I dragged my feet as I walked to the school building. Halfway across the sunny playground, I suddenly smiled as I imagined the next plane buzzing over the school compound bringing another brown sugar box from home.

* * *

Recently, my mom shared, "We were fortunate that planes came often to our station. I mailed something to you each time."

Mom, this story is to honor you for unfailingly showing your love long distance through letters and cookies from home.

– 23 –

The Traveling Leaf

Adrienne N. Wartts

I won't pretend to understand God's mysterious ways, but I know He is always working behind the scenes to bring miracles to fruition. This story is an example of a miracle that followed my beloved father's earthly departure after a courageous battle with a memory loss disease. It also serves as an example of how my mother and I chose to honor him.

A few days after my father passed, it was time to decide on his final resting place. That Sunday, my mother and I set out to visit two cemeteries—one based on where my father's sister Rose was laid to rest, and the other based on proximity.

The Journey

The cemetery nearest to my parent's home looked like a lovely garden. At the entry point stood a grand triumphal arch and an elongated, Roman-style pool with a running fountain as the centerpiece. During the drive, I slowed my speed so my mother could have a better view from the street.

"Let's skip this for now and go to the one where Rose is buried first," my mother said. "But I want to come back here, because I think this is the one." I could hear and feel my mother mourning while she peered out the window as we passed by. "It's beautiful. And I want my husband to have the best."

As we approached the entry of the cemetery where my aunt Rose was buried, we were greeted with a Gothic stone marker at the gate. We drove around the block-long cemetery. It was like a maze with its plethora of winding roads lined with an abundance of oak, maple, and hickory trees.

Leaves

The driveways were full of piles of crisp brown, tan, and yellow leaves. "I would just drive over them," my mother said.

"Well, let's see," I said as I proceeded. Then I heard a noise beneath the car. "I think I'm dragging leaves along."

I hurriedly put the car in "park" before I noticed the tightness of the space at the corner of the narrow pathway. I stepped out and, sure enough, a mound of leaves was accompanying us. I gently kicked away as many as I could. When I reentered the car, I looked at the pile of leaves blocking the road in front of us. It also partially blocked the turn I needed to make and was much larger than the pile I'd just tried to drive over. I needed to carefully maneuver so I wouldn't drag more leaves, back the car into the iron gate, or bump against the huge tree at the corner of the turn.

By the time I finished repeatedly backing up then moving forward inch by inch and turning the steering wheel bit by bit, we both figured we'd seen and been through enough for the day. Fortunately, it was easy to vacate the maze. We were only one turn and two blocks from the exit.

"Let's look at the other cemetery later," my mother said. "And let's come back here when the office is open so we can find out where Rose is buried. Maybe your father can be placed close to her."

"I think he'd like that," I said.

The Reflection

When we made it back inside the house, I noticed a smooth brown leaf in its entirety lying beside my suitcase. It had apparently fallen from the hem of my jeans. "Look," I said to my mother as I held it in front of me. "This leaf made it all the way back here with us."

My mother smiled and then pointed to one of the two collages of dried leaves hanging on the wall in the foyer. "That leaf looks closest to the leaf at the top on the right in that collage you gave us."

I walked over to the collage and placed the leaf on the table beneath it. "It sure does."

Years ago, my mother asked me to make her a collage of dried leaves. I made a trip to the botanical garden, gathered a variety of fallen leaves, dried them, and positioned them in frames. A few weeks later, I presented the collages to my parents.

"Oh, those are beautiful," my mother said. "Look at the shades of brown, red, orange, and yellow!"

My father was beside her on the couch. "Those are nice, very nice," he said. "Why don't we hang one on each side of that mirror?"

My mother and I agreed. Then my father promptly hung two collages in the foyer and one in their bedroom.

The Miracle

That Tuesday, once my mother and I returned to the cemetery, I called the office to ask about the location of my aunt's plot.

A woman walked out to meet us. "It's two blocks past our office," she said as she circled the location on a map. "Make the first right turn. It's just before Walnut Street." She handed the map to my mother. "Be careful. There's a board over the plot being prepared."

On the way, I noticed all the piles of leaves had been collected. When we reached our destination, my mother said, "This is exactly where we were the other day!"

"Yeah, right at that corner," I said as I approached my aunt's plot. What I saw surprised me. "The plot next to Aunt Rose's is already marked with Daddy's name! Did you tell them that's where you wanted him to be placed?"

"No." My mother was just as surprised. "I haven't talked to anyone here yet."

"Well, who arranged it?"

"I have no idea."

My eyes became damp as I remembered the leaf at the house. I believed where we were was where my father would have wanted to be laid to rest, directly next to his beloved sister. Proverbs 16:9 says, *We can make our plans, but the LORD determines our steps* (NLT). I knew God was watching the entire scene and that He directed it.

"That leaf came from this vicinity. That's why it felt so special the other day," I said as I looked at my mother. "I think if Daddy could chime in, he'd want to be here."

She smiled. "Yes."

We didn't visit the other cemetery. We honored the decision that had already been made.

– 24 –

The King Honors His Best Friend

A Children's Story from 2 Samuel 9

Terrie Hellard-Brown

Do you have a best friend? I don't have one because I'm a lizard. I'm too busy doing lizardy things to have a best friend. One of my favorite things to do is sneaking into the King's palace to see what's going on. As a lizard, I have sticky feet and can hang out on the wall unnoticed by most people except for the King's youngest son who likes to try to catch me. But I outsmart him all the time.

King David had a best friend named Jonathan, but he died. King David was very sad, of course. He didn't just feel sad. He wanted to honor Jonathan. You know, after seeing how much David loved Jonathan,

I might consider having a best friend someday.

David loved his friend so much he wanted to find a way to keep his promise to Jonathan. He promised that Jonathan's family would always be taken care of when David became king. So, you know what he did? He asked Jonathan's helper if anyone was left in Jonathan's family that he could honor and bless. The helper said only one son was left, and his name was Mephi—Mephibo—Mephiblo—

Mephibosheth! That's it. Have you ever heard of such a name? Can I just call him Mephy for short?

He was a young father who couldn't walk. In our time, people who couldn't walk often were not treated well, so the fact that David honored him by asking him to become part of his family and to eat at his table for the rest of his life was a pretty major thing!

Not only did Mephy eat at the King's table, King David gave him all of his family's land and appointed the helper's family to farm the land and take care of it for Mephy. Isn't that amazing?

He honored Jonathan by keeping his promise to him.

He honored Jonathan by respecting his family name.

He honored Jonathan by accepting his son whom others might reject.

He honored Jonathan by returning his family's land and blessing his child and grandchild.

Mostly, he honored Jonathan by obeying God and doing good to others.

I've never seen a person have such—how do you say it? *Umm*—oh yes, *integrity*. If I ever do have a best friend, I hope he and I have that kind of love and integrity toward each other. How about you?

Index of Authors

Meet the Authors

Dian Avila

Dian lives in South San Jose with her husband, Jose. They served overseas for ten years as missionaries, and her husband still travels throughout Latin America. They have three adult children and four grandchildren. Dian enjoys encouraging others as an assistant principal at Legacy Christian School. She also delights in spending time with family and traveling.

Debra Celovsky

Debra Celovsky has served in pastoral ministry most of her adult life. Her devotionals and articles have appeared in a number of publications. She is on the board of Inspire Christian Writers, and Chair of the Editorial Team for the Inspire Anthology. Her banana cream pie is famous amongst friends and family. She blogs through the One Year Bible at debracelovsky.com.

Kelly Conley

Kelly became a Christian in 1994 and, since taking a creative writing class in 2008, has been writing devotionals, nature pieces, and children's short stories. After retiring from State service in May of 2022, she joined Inspire Christian Writers. She has also joined a writer's critique group and is happy to be working on her writing projects.

Christine Hagion

Christine loved writing as a child, and that passion has never left. An ordained minister, she writes stories, poems, songs, and plays. Her blog, In the Spirit of Thomas Aquinas, offers snippets of life experience and personal insights into how faith can help us navigate the trials in life: christinehagion.com.

Terrie Hellard-Brown

Terrie writes devotionals and children's stories. Her podcast, *Books that Spark,* reviews kids' books for parents. Her blog discusses being Christ's disciple while discipling children. Terrie uses her experiences as a mother, missionary, minister, and teacher to speak to the hearts of readers.

Joyce D. Hightower

Joyce Dixon Hightower writes books and songs to inspire others to be fervent in their service of love. Her works reveal a trove of world experiences including local and international medical careers, being a single mother of three and a grandma of five, and founding an international non-profit supporting orphans and widows.

Lainey La Shay

Lainey La Shay is a writer who shines light on the deep issues of life and relationships. She boldly shares her own experiences to bring hope to others and awareness to issues that are difficult to discuss, such as domestic violence. While she can't show you her face or tell you her real name, Lainey is passionate about being a champion for those who have faced insurmountable odds. She wants to help them come out the other side standing tall.

Lenette Lindsey

Lenette Lindsey is a Bible teacher, writer, and graduate from Dallas Theological Seminary who deeply loves Jesus and people. When not writing, she's glamping with her husband in Texas. They have three grown children—Braedon, Bryce, and Madison. Don't miss a thing by joining her at lenettelindsey.com.

Malcolm Mackinnon

Malcolm is an affable Brit, capable of humor and cynicism in equal measures. He ministers in the Bay Area as a children's pastor, with his long-suffering wife, Donna, and two astonishing adopted children. He is just as happy writing books on theology as he is scripting sitcoms.

Maureen Miller

Maureen Miller is an award-winning author who writes for Guideposts and several online devotional sites. She enjoys life with her husband and their three children—and grandchildren— on Selah Farm, their hobby homestead in North Carolina. She blogs at penningpansies.com, sharing God's extraordinary character in the ordinary things of life.

Robyn Mulder

Robyn Mulder lives in South Dakota with her husband, Gary. They often go to Lincoln, Nebraska to visit their four children and two precious grandchildren. Robyn writes about faith and mental health at robynmulder.com. She also encourages others with her "Catch Your Thoughts with Robyn Mulder" podcast.

Kimberly Novak

Kimberly dedicates her time as a wife, mother, author, and spiritual director. Her passion for inspiring and motivating those on a spiritual journey has bloomed into various ministries. Kimberly writes inspirational gems, all for God's glory. View her blog and other writings at kimberlynovak.com.

Anita Peluso

Anita Peluso began writing devotionals on Instagram two years ago after graduating with an MA in Biblical Studies, but dreams of writing a historical fiction novel. She lives in Western Washington with her husband, two cats, four ducks and seven chickens.

Janelle Roselli

Janelle writes YA Fantasy and Adult Speculative Fiction. In both genres, she enjoys exploring the themes of life after death and the power of redemption. When not writing, Janelle can be found obsessing over her two rescue pups, planning her next trip, or occasionally besting her husband at golf.

Darcy Schock

Darcy Schock is a girl who loves stories. In fact, she writes stories for people who want more hope in a brighter tomorrow and more freedom to unlock the person God created them to be. She is a small-town country girl who loves coffee and the smell of new books. She has been married over ten years to her high school sweetheart and has three daughters. They live nestled in a grove of trees in central Illinois.

Debbie Jones Warren

Debbie writes memoir about her childhood in a boarding school in Nigeria where her parents were missionaries. Her devotions and short stories are published in *The Upper Room, Chicken Soup for the Soul, Inspire,* and other anthologies. She leads a writers' group in the Bay Area, and blogs at debbiejoneswarren.com

Adrienne N. Wartts

Adrienne N. Wartts recently answered God's call to shift her focus to faith-based writing and editing, and has had the opportunity to contribute to *Our Daily Bread*'s VOICES brand. She holds an MA in American culture studies from Washington University, and currently resides in Massachusetts.

Karen Wood

Karen D. Wood, L.C.S.W., is a neurotherapist, inviting readers to learn about the impact of trauma on the brain, body, and behavior and how to find healing through learning about the Creator of it all. She has written *Brain Prayers: Explore Your Brain, Expand Your Prayers*. Current work: developing nationwide trauma training for churches.

About Inspire Christian Writers

Inspire Christian Writers is a nonprofit organization whose sole reason for existing is to equip and encourage writers, no matter where you are in your writing career. Started in California, Inspire now has members from multiple countries and across the US. And what was begun as a simple writing group has developed into a comprehensive organization meeting the needs of writers in numerous ways:

- Our award-winning blog and website, (named a top ten world-wide resource for Christian writers!)
- Online and in-person critique groups
- Writing Contests
- Directory of vetted professionals serving writers, with discounts!
- Workshops, both in-person and online
- Networking opportunities
- Writing credits (via our blog, contests, anthology, etc.)
- Discounts for members to some conferences, events, and contests
- Annual anthology
- And the Vision Christian Writers conference at Mt. Hermon (vcwconf.com ... with a discount larger than Inspire's annual membership fee.)

If you are interested in joining Inspire, or want information on our current events and offerings, please visit inspirewriters.com.

We look forward to welcoming you into our family!

Previous Anthologies from Inspire Christian Writers

Inspire Trust (2012)

Inspire Faith (2013)

Friends of Inspire Faith (2013)

Inspired Glimpses of God's Presence (2013)

Inspire Victory (2014)

Inspire Promise (2014)

Inspire Forgiveness (2015)

Inspire Joy (2016)

Inspire Love (2017)

Inspire Kindness (2018)

Inspire Grace (2019)

Inspire Community (2021)

Inspire Courage (2022)

Made in the USA
Middletown, DE
28 December 2023

45656569R00106